Jenna swa[...]**his chest. "Yo**[...]**t."**

"Why?"

"I barely know you."

"You knew enough about me to find me on the beach and save me from an assassin. I reckon that gives us a pass on convention."

She rested her forehead against his chest. "I didn't come to Cancun to get involved with a man." But, boy, had that backfired on her.

"And I have no business getting involved with you." He gripped her shoulders and set her at arm's length. "As a SEAL, I'm gone more than I'm home. And with an assassin after me, I can't risk you becoming collateral damage."

NAVY SEAL CAPTIVE

New York Times Bestselling Author

ELLE JAMES

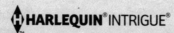
HARLEQUIN® INTRIGUE®

This book is dedicated to my sister, Delilah Devlin, who was an officer in the US army. She has inspired me to be the best I can be in my military career and in my journey to publication. She's my mentor, sounding board and critique partner. And she isn't afraid to tell me like it is. I love you, Sis!

ISBN-13: 978-0-373-69898-1

Navy SEAL Captive

Copyright © 2016 by Mary Jernigan

Recycling programs for this product may not exist in your area.

Printed in U.S.A.

www.Harlequin.com

Elle James, a *New York Times* bestselling author, started writing when her sister challenged her to write a romance novel. She has managed a full-time job and raised three wonderful children, and she and her husband even tried ranching exotic birds (ostriches, emus and rheas). Ask her, and she'll tell you what it's like to go toe-to-toe with an angry 350-pound bird! Elle loves to hear from fans at ellejames@earthlink.net or ellejames.com.

CAST OF CHARACTERS

Sawyer Houston—Highly trained, skilled gunner and navy SEAL from SEAL Boat Team 22 on vacation in Cancun. Secretly he is the son of a US senator.

Jenna Broyles—Jilted at the altar, she's determined to be anything but boring while on her "honeymoon" in Cancun.

Dutton "Duff" Calloway—Highly trained, skilled demolitions expert and navy SEAL from SEAL Boat Team 22 on vacation in Cancun.

Benjamin "Montana" Raines—Expert sniper and navy SEAL from SEAL Boat Team 22 on vacation in Cancun.

Quentin Lovett—Highly trained, expertly skilled weapons specialist and navy SEAL from SEAL Boat Team 22 on vacation in Cancun.

Natalie Layne—Stealth Operations Specialists agent with special sniper skills, on vacation in Cancun after rescuing her sister from a human trafficking attempt.

Lance Johnson—Stealth Operations Specialists agent with highly evolved computer and technical skills useful in field operations.

Carmelo Devita—Mexican drug lord also involved in human trafficking and known to hire out mercenaries.

Jorge Ramirez—Thug working for Carmelo Devita.

Becca Smith—Vacationing beauty who befriends Jenna.

Trey Danner—Former FBI special agent who's worked undercover with a stateside drug dealer.

Carly Samuels—The friend Jenna brought along on her "honeymoon."

Rand Houston—US senator and self-made millionaire who clawed his way to a huge fortune in the oil and gas industry.

Chapter One

"Seriously. I can't believe you talked me into this. And to go straight for the biggest first? Isn't that pushing it?" Sawyer Houston adjusted the web seat and waited his turn on the platform. Perched on the edge of a two-hundred-foot cliff, staring down into the vast jungle, Sawyer balked. Cancún Adventures boasted the longest, most exciting zip line in Mexico, guaranteed to make you scream. Not, in Sawyer's opinion, the most reassuring advertisement.

"It's not like you to turn away from a challenge, Houston," Quentin Lovett ribbed. "You've fast-roped out of helicopters, entered buildings full of terrorists and been shot at by rifles, machine guns and mortars." Quentin snorted. "What's a little ol' zip line gonna hurt?"

"I don't know who set it up, whether the cable is strong enough to withstand my weight or if there's a way to stop me at the other end. Hell, I can't see the other end, and plunging into a tree at the bottom isn't my idea of fun. Besides, how would that look on my tombstone? 'SEAL ends his navy career on vacation, sliding to his death on a poorly rigged zip line.'"

"Step aside." Quentin circled Sawyer. "Let me show you how it's done."

"That's right. Test the line. I'll be sure to send your

mother a letter telling of your bravery in the face of a zip line."

A couple of women stood in front of Quentin. The curvy one in the khaki shorts and white Cancún T-shirt shook her head, her dark red curls bouncing with her nervous movements. "No. I've changed my mind." She backed away from her friend with the short dark hair, running into Quentin.

"Whoa, darlin'." Quentin steadied her, his brows rose and he winked at Sawyer.

"Sorry." Her cheeks bloomed with color, and she hurriedly stepped away from him.

"Jenna, you have to do it," the dark-haired, petite woman said. "It's part of your kick-the-boring therapy."

"Yeah, but I was thinking more along the lines of riding a roller coaster, not speeding through the jungle at Mach ten on a cable probably salvaged from a shipyard by people who might have used office staples to nail it to some tree ready to fall over at any minute."

Sawyer took a breath for Jenna. How one woman could say all that without inhaling was beyond him. But she was kind of cute, and he didn't blame her for her trepidation.

"Hey, I'll go first to test it out," the other woman said.

"No way, Carly. If you die, I'm stranded in the jungle with no one to get me back to the hotel to find my lost luggage."

Sawyer's lips quirked at the redhead's adamant refusal to participate in the death-defying feat of zip-lining. "I'll give you a ride."

Jenna shot him a narrow-eyed glance before turning back to her friend. "Or you'll be leaving me at the mercy of strangers, possibly mass murderers."

The brunette rolled her eyes, then gave Sawyer a considering look. "He's not a mass murderer, and he's really cute. You could do worse. Now, I'm going. I'll see you back at the parking lot." She pulled on the gloves they'd been given and stepped up to the man in charge.

The man in the red Cancún Adventures T-shirt and black cotton shorts stubbed out his cigarette and hooked her belt to the cable. "If you want to slow, grab the cable with your glove. But don't do it too soon, or you will stop in the middle of the cable," he said in heavily accented English.

"Here's to shaking it off and plotting a more adventurous course in your life." The brunette leaned toward the cliff.

Jenna swayed toward her friend. "Carly, don't—" But she was too late. Carly leaped off the cliff and raced toward the jungle at breakneck speed, squealing in delight.

Quentin chuckled. "Damn, she beat me to it." He turned toward Sawyer. "Are you going to let a girl shame you?"

Sawyer crossed his arms over his chest. "There's no shame in preferring to keep my bones intact."

The redhead nodded, her gaze on her friend as she disappeared into the dark green jungle below. "That's what I told Carly." She glanced back at Sawyer. "Don't get me wrong. I'm all for adventure." Jenna bit her lip. "Or, at least, that was the point of this exercise." Turning toward the cliff, she straightened her shoulders. "And, for the record, I'm not boring."

"Didn't say you were. Actually, you're far from it," Sawyer agreed, admiring her curvy figure and the shock of auburn hair that refused to be contained in the ponytail.

Quentin performed a sweeping bow in front of the woman. "Allow me."

"Sure. I'm not in a hurry to plunge to my death." She stepped back, this time bumping into Sawyer.

He wrapped an arm around her, absorbed the impact

of her body and breathed in the flowery scent of her hair. Nope. Not boring at all. With her small body pressed close to his, he forgot all about the zip line and his argument with Quentin.

"Sorry," she mumbled and stepped to his side and out of his embrace, her cheeks flushing a soft pink.

Everywhere she'd touched him still resonated with the warmth of her body. Sawyer's groin tightened.

"Nothing to it." Quentin allowed the attendant to hook his D-ring to the pulley and held on to the cable with his gloved hand. "See you at the bottom, if you have the guts to do it." He winked, lifted his legs and took off, sliding to his doom in the jungle, whooping and hollering as he went.

Jenna drew in a long breath and let it out on a sigh. "I did come to Cancún to start over and be more adventurous."

Sawyer smiled. "You don't have to do the zip line to be adventurous."

"No?" She glanced at him hopefully, her face brightening. Then her brows drew together, and she stiffened. "Yeah, but I don't ever want to be accused of being boring again."

"I take it someone called you boring," Sawyer said.

She lifted her chin. "My ex-fiancé."

"He must have been blind."

"And a cheating bastard." She stepped up to the attendant. "I'm going."

"You want me to go with you?" Sawyer offered.

She shook her head. "No. I'll be fine. If Carly can do it, so can I." Jenna stared at the attendant, biting her lip. "I'm ready."

The attendant gave her the same instructions he'd given to Quentin and Carly.

Jenna closed her eyes and said, "Could you give me a

little push?" Her hands shook on the line hooked to the pulley as she drew in a ragged breath.

The attendant nodded, a smile teasing the corners of his mouth, and gave her a hefty shove. Her small body flew out over the cliff and raced to the bottom. A long, high-pitched scream ripped through the air, fading the farther away she went.

"Damn." Sawyer checked his nylon web belt, which fit snugly around his legs, and stepped up to the attendant. "Guess I'm going, too."

He turned to the man behind him, hoping that one last person would talk him out of taking the plunge.

The tall, muscular man with light brown hair and steely gray eyes stared right through him.

Nope. There'd be no help on that front.

When he stepped up to the edge, the attendant blocked him with his hand. "Wait until the senoriita makes it to the bottom."

The attendant waited a full minute before he snapped Sawyer's link onto the line, repeated the instructions and left Sawyer teetering on the edge of the cliff, praying the cable held and the glove would do its job and slow his descent. In the back of his mind, he hoped that he'd find the woman he'd held in his arms for that brief second to thank her for shaming him into jumping off a cliff when his gut told him he was crazy.

He jumped.

Sawyer fell into the jungle, his speed picking up as he swished past treetops, the wind clearing his head and sharpening his mind. As he dropped below the canopy of trees, he could make out the base and Quentin standing at the bottom.

But he wasn't slowing, and at the pace he was going, he'd crash into the pole at the bottom. How had he let his teammate talk him into sliding down a cable he hadn't personally inspected? If he lived through this, he'd have a word or two with Quentin.

He gripped the line with his gloved hand, slowing a little, enough to give him a slight amount of reassurance he could stop himself before he crashed into the pole at the other end. For the first time since he jumped off the upper platform, he glanced around at the jungle below. When he looked back at his destination, his heart leaped.

The distance closed faster than he expected and before he knew it, he was careening the last fifty feet into the base. Sawyer grabbed the cable with the gloved hand and squeezed. The wind no longer whipped past him, and his descent slowed the closer he came to the bottom. He couldn't remember being that terrified since his first fast-rope experience out of a fully operational helicopter hovering thirty feet from the ground.

Ten feet from his feet touching the ground, the cable jolted in his hand. Sawyer bounced in the harness and then dropped like a ton of bricks to the ground. He tucked and rolled, absorbing the impact, and then sprang to his feet. What the hell had just happened?

The attendant at the bottom yelled something in Spanish and threw himself into the jungle. Quentin followed suit.

Sawyer spun in time to see the cable springing back toward him, detached from the pole at the other end. He dived to the right and ducked behind a tree. The cable whipped through the treetops like an angry snake and finally lay still on the ground.

His heart pounding like a bass drum, Sawyer leaped to his feet and yelled, "Everyone okay?"

Quentin climbed out of the brush, pulling leaves out of his hair. "Holy crap. Did you see that?"

Sawyer's jaw tightened, and he forced himself to take a deep breath. "Saw and felt it."

"If you'd been a couple seconds later on that cable…" Quentin shook his head and clapped Sawyer on the back. "Damn, buddy. I hate it when you're right."

Sawyer brushed the dirt off his hands. "In this case, I wish I hadn't been right."

While the zip-line attendant scrambled to his feet, swearing in Spanish, Sawyer unbuckled the nylon straps from around his legs and let the harness drop. "Next time you want me to slide down a zip line…"

Quentin held up his hands. "Don't worry. There won't be a next time." He felt his pockets and cursed. Then he dived into the brush and came up with his cell phone. "The good news is I got it all on video. The guys are gonna die when they see this."

Sawyer snorted. "I almost died living it."

Quentin shoved the phone into his pocket and turned toward the exit. "I have to admit, I was surprised to see you coming. But even more surprised when the redhead came down first."

Sawyer glanced around and didn't see the woman named Jenna anywhere. "I take it Jenna arrived safely at the bottom."

"She did. She and her pretty friend left, claimed they needed to get back to find a piece of missing luggage. The redhead told me to tell you thanks for the encouragement."

Disappointed he'd missed her, but glad she'd gone before him when the cable was still intact, Sawyer asked, "You didn't happen to catch her full name, did you?"

"She didn't offer a last name." Quentin turned back to Sawyer. "Why? Are you interested?"

Again, Sawyer shrugged. "Just wondered." Hell, yes,

he was interested, but he'd be damned if he let Quentin know. He'd pick at him incessantly.

"I did get her roommate's name, though." Quentin patted his smartphone. "Carly Samuels. We have a date tonight."

Figured. Quentin didn't waste time when it came to women. He was a charmer, and women fell for him all the time. Perhaps the best-looking man on the team with his black hair and ice-blue eyes, he usually had his pick of the ladies.

Quentin had a date and Duff was with his lady friend, Natalie, leaving Sawyer and Montana fending for themselves for dinner and drinks. Which suited Sawyer just fine. Montana was a big, outdoorsy mountain man who didn't say much but was good company. They had a week and a half left of their two weeks in Cancún. Granted, he loved his SEAL teammates like brothers, but he could use a little quality time away from them, preferably in the company of someone of the opposite sex.

As they slid into the rented Jeep, Quentin turned to Sawyer. "You had a few minutes alone with her. Why didn't you get her name and number? We could have gone on a double date."

"We weren't alone. The attendant was there. And who said I wanted to go out with her, anyway?" And he sure as hell wouldn't go on a double date with Quentin. No, if Sawyer had gotten Jenna's number, he'd have taken her out alone. Maybe for a walk along the beach in the moonlight. If she showed even the slightest interest, he might have stolen a kiss. Those pretty pink lips she'd chewed on prior to taking the big leap on the zip line were full and plump. Made for kissing.

"You've got to get out there, be more sociable, network and sell yourself."

Sawyer's fingers tightened on the steering wheel at Quentin's comment. He'd heard the same words from his father's mouth on more than one occasion. Quentin was right. He hadn't dated in a while, and he was getting rusty at socializing with women.

What Quentin and his father never understood was that Sawyer didn't like being in the limelight. Especially in front of all of his father's peers. He'd rather be the best he could be at his job in the navy SEALs, the one place he'd proven he was good enough to make the cut. Besides, wearing the uniform was usually all he needed to find a date when he really wanted one. Too bad he was in civvies here.

"So do you have plans for tonight?" Quentin asked.

"Yeah. I plan on spending the afternoon on the beach. Maybe I'll rent a WaveRunner. Then I'm going to eat seafood and have a few beers with Montana. I don't have to live for excitement like you."

Quentin shook his head. "Since excitement seems to follow us, you might need a little rest and relaxation." He linked his hands behind his neck. "Missions always leave me wired, ready to expend some energy."

"Like winding the springs on a watch?"

"Yeah. Something like that."

"Not me. We've spent the past few months either training or performing back-to-back missions. I could use some downtime to regroup and get my head on straight."

"Well, you do your thing. I'll do mine." Quentin shot a grin his way. "With the adventurous and beautiful Carly."

Sawyer almost opened his mouth and asked Quentin to secure the phone number for Carly's friend Jenna. Then he thought better of it. He didn't need Quentin to find him a woman. If he really wanted to go out with her, he'd find her himself. She had to be somewhere in Cancún. The resort area wasn't that big. He might even run into her on the beach.

His pulse quickened at the thought.

EVEN AFTER THE long drive back to the resort, Jenna Broyles still shook from her experience on the zip line.

"I can't believe you actually did it," Carly said for the tenth time as she got out of the rental car and met Jenna in front of the hood. "I'm so proud of you." She hugged her and stood beaming like a mother bird on her chick's first flight. "So how does it feel to be adventurous?"

Jenna pressed a hand to her belly. "A little nauseating."

Carly laughed. "You'll get over it. Just like you'll get over being stood up at the altar."

That reminder bit into Jenna's newfound adventurous spirit. Though it had been almost two months since she'd stood in the anteroom at the church, wondering where Audra, her maid of honor, was and waiting for her cue to walk down the aisle, it still hurt that her groom hadn't bothered to come to his own wedding. He'd not only failed to appear but also run off with the maid of honor.

Jenna had been adjusting the veil over her hair, wishing her mother could have lived to be there at her wedding, when the text had come through.

Sorry. Can't make the wedding. Changed my mind. Keep the tickets for the honeymoon.

She'd stood dry-eyed, shocked and unable to comprehend what had happened, until her father came through the door to lead her down the aisle. One look at her face and he'd grabbed the phone from her hand.

After a few choice words, he'd hustled her out of the church into the waiting limousine and taken her to the home she'd grown up in, where she could lick her wounds. Carly had done the honors of sending everyone home and canceling the reception and wedding band. She'd joined Jenna and her father at the ranch, ready to take one of the rifles over the mantel to Tyler's lying, cheating heart.

Jenna had heard through the grapevine that Tyler had slept with Jenna's former best friend, Audra, on the night of his bachelor party. He claimed Audra was more fun than his boring bride, and he couldn't go through with the wedding knowing he'd be stuck in a mundane marriage for the rest of his life.

Jenna had planned her wedding for the date her parents had been married in February. But as an accountant, she couldn't plan their honeymoon until after tax season. She'd almost forfeited her tickets until Carly talked her into going. She needed to show Tyler and, more important, herself that she wasn't boring. She knew how to be adventurous.

Of course, she had to take Carly along with her to show her how to do it.

Carly pulled in front of the resort hotel, shifted into Park and got out.

"Aren't you going to park it yourself?" Jenna asked. "I don't mind walking a little."

Carly clucked her tongue. "Don't be so tight. We're only here for ten days. You might as well live a little. Let the valet park it for us." Her friend tilted her head. "Come on. It won't kill you to be a bit extravagant."

"I just don't like spending when I don't need to," Jenna grumbled as she got out of the vehicle and joined Carly on the sidewalk.

Carly handed over the keys to the valet and sauntered into the hotel.

Once inside, Jenna eyed the front desk. "I'm going to ask whether my suitcase has arrived."

"Okay. I'll go on up and be first in the shower. I have a date with Quentin tonight." Carly frowned. "You don't mind, do you?"

Jenna did mind. She didn't enjoy eating alone in a restaurant. But she didn't want to hold Carly back from having fun. "I don't mind at all. I was thinking of splurging, like you said, and ordering room service and soaking in that incredible hot tub."

"Mmm." Carly grinned. "Sounds great. And I'll definitely want to be out of the room when you do it. That's one disadvantage to having the bridal suite. It was meant to be shared with your lover, not your girlfriend." She winked. "You should order champagne and do it right."

"Why? It's not like I'm celebrating."

"Yes, you are." Carly hooked her arm and marched her toward the concierge. "You're celebrating your liberation from marrying the wrong guy." She stopped and faced the concierge. "We'd like to order a lovely bottle of champagne delivered to the bridal suite."

"No, really." Jenna's face heated. "It's not necessary."

The man behind the counter stared from Carly to Jenna and back. "Which is it to be?"

Carly shook her head. "Champagne to the bridal suite within the next twenty minutes." She named a brand that Jenna hoped was on the cheaper end of the wine list. "Thank you." She grabbed Jenna's hand and tugged her toward the elevator. "Come on. You have some hot-tubbing to do."

Jenna dug her feet into the tile floor. "I will, but I need to check on my missing luggage."

Carly let go of her hand and nodded. "That's right. And I was headed for the shower and a date." She saluted. "I'll see you in the suite. I hope your bag came in." Her overwhelmingly cheerful friend spun away and disappeared into the elevator.

Jenna waited at the bellman's stand next to the registration desk. A rush of young people converged on the desk, tying up the bellmen and the clerks. A gentleman stood close to the bellman's stand, tapping his toe impatiently as he checked into the hotel.

Jenna could see everyone was busy and figured it would take time for anyone to free up and help her. Prepared to return later, she spotted her hard-sided gray case between the registration counter and the bellman's desk.

Excited that her suitcase had finally arrived, she scooped it up and headed for the elevator, saving the bellman one more person to deal with. Glad to have the case with her dinner clothes inside it, now she could relax and enjoy the rest of her "honeymoon."

As she stepped into the elevator, she thought of Carly and the man she'd just met at the zip-line excursion. Was her friend brave or foolish to go out with a man she knew nothing about?

Deep down, Jenna wished the man called Sawyer had asked for her number or asked to take her out on a date while in Cancún. She and Carly could have double-dated with the two men.

Perhaps she was being silly, but she'd thought she'd felt a connection with him. The warmth of his body at her back, the security of his arm around her waist.

Was she so desperate to be with a man, she had started reading into things? Hadn't she learned with Tyler that men weren't attracted to women like her? Or at least not for long. She was too boring, afraid to take risks, stuck in her ways.

Jenna tugged the rubber band out of her hair and shook her unruly curls loose. Well, maybe it was time to be more daring. She'd ask Carly to get the number for her date's friend.

In the meantime, Jenna had a date with a bottle of champagne and a hot tub.

Funny thing was…she didn't even like champagne.

No sooner had she entered her room than Carly stepped out of the shower. "I'm done if you want to rinse off," she called out. The door to the bathroom stood wide-open. Carly leaned against the counter, applying makeup, her slim, athletic body wrapped in a towel.

"No, I'll wait for the hot tub," Jenna said and set her case on the floor.

"The champagne beat you here. Help yourself. I already poured a glass." She turned and raised her glass, then drank a sip of the sparkling liquid.

Jenna figured that since it was paid for, she might as well try to enjoy it and poured a glass. She carried it to the huge floor-to-ceiling windows overlooking the ocean. The sun was still up, shining over the water. People crowded the beach, some swimming, others soaking up the sun. Families corralled children, and lovers lay entwined on towels, smooching as if they were the only ones on the beach.

Sighing, Jenna downed a long gulp of the bubbly liquid. This would have been her and Tyler's honeymoon had he gone through with the marriage.

Now, two months after the horrible embarrassment of being jilted at the altar, she was glad she hadn't married Tyler. They might already have been divorced or had the wedding annulled. Jenna would never have been happy with him. They were too different. She wanted a man who could be faithful. He wasn't.

The ping of a cell phone sounded from the bathroom.

"Whoops." Carly raced out of the bathroom, fluffing her short, dark, damp hair. She threw on a powder-blue sundress and strappy stilettoes and grabbed her purse. "Quentin is waiting for me downstairs."

"Isn't it early to go to dinner?" Jenna stared out at the beach.

"He wants to take me driving around first. Then we're going to walk on the beach. After that, we'll do dinner and dancing." She smiled. "He wants to get to know me." Carly hugged Jenna and bussed her cheek. "Don't do anything I wouldn't, and enjoy your hot tub and champagne."

"I will." Jenna sighed as Carly hurried out, the door closing automatically behind her.

As soon as the door closed, Jenna cursed. She'd meant to ask Carly to get the phone number for Quentin's friend.

She teetered on the balls of her feet, tempted to run after her friend, but didn't. For a long moment Jenna stared at that door as if it were a barrier to her self-esteem.

Why was she staying in her room, soaking in a tub, when she could be out, enjoying the sunshine and salty air? Wasn't she there to be adventurous? What better way than to go outside and experience life?

Scrapping the idea of a long soak in the hot tub, she stripped down to her underwear and slung her case up on the bed. She refused to hide in the honeymoon suite when she could be out having fun. With a determined flip of her hair, she flicked the latches. They didn't open. Funny. She hadn't locked them, knowing airport security would want to inspect for illegal or potentially dangerous items. Hell, she hadn't thought to bring the key. And yet somehow, the locks had engaged.

She fished in her purse for her metal file and went to work jimmying the locks one at a time until finally they each sprang open. Jenna straightened triumphantly. One more hurdle overcome. She could do anything when she set her mind to it. "Boring… Ha!"

Jenna flung open the case, ready to pull out her sexy black dress.

For a moment, she stared into the case, her mind slow to realize this wasn't her case at all.

"Oh no." On top was a layer of clothing. Dark trousers, dark, long-sleeved T-shirts, a black ski mask. Things she would expect to see in a case bound for the ski slopes or a really cold climate, not the tropics.

Jenna closed the case and stared down at it, wondering what to do with it. There was no luggage tag on the outside identifying the owner should the case be lost.

Feeling guilty already about forcing the case open, she lifted the lid and glanced inside again. Maybe there was some form of identification buried inside.

Carefully lifting the clothes, she set them aside on the bed. Beneath the clothing was nothing. Strangely, the case still seemed heavy, and it was deeper on the outside than the inside. Was there a false bottom? She ran her hand around the inside of the case, searching for a lever or button to push. Finally she found it, sliding the device to the left. The divider popped up enough that she could slip her fingers beneath it and lift.

Jenna gasped.

Parts of what appeared to be a rifle lay disassembled in a bed of foam, including the stock, butt, scope and bolt. A manila envelope lay on top of the weapon.

Why would a man need to bring his gun to Cancún? Was he part of a marksman team?

Her stomach knotting, Jenna refused to think past this being a competitive marksman's prize rifle. With no other identification to be found, she lifted the envelope, hoping to find the owner's name and cell phone number inside.

Flipping up the prongs on the metal clasp, she opened it and spilled the contents onto the bed.

Photographs, money and a note lay on the comforter.

She examined the wad of cash secured by a rubber band and counted fifty one-hundred-dollar bills. Holy crap. Five thousand dollars. Her knees trembled. Who carried around five thousand dollars in cash?

Jenna picked up the photographs, her eyes widening. The man in the picture had dark hair and dark eyes. He was nice-looking, dressed in dark jeans and a black T-shirt. The material of the shirt stretched over broad, muscular shoulders. Tattoos peeked from beneath the sleeves.

Jenna peered closer, her breath catching in her throat. She recognized the man in the photo as the man she'd met on the zip-line platform not an hour earlier.

Her hand shaking, she unfolded the note. Her pulse slowed and her blood turned cold.

Bring him to the agreed-upon location by 9:00 p.m. Dead or alive.

A lead weight sank to the pit of Jenna's belly. She'd wanted adventure, but not this much. At that moment, she'd settle for being boring Jenna.

Chapter Two

When Sawyer returned to the resort, he went to the bungalow he'd rented for his two-week stay, shed his jeans and pulled on a pair of swim trunks. After sweating in the humidity of the jungle, he could think of nothing he'd rather do than go for a dip in the ocean.

Grabbing a towel, he headed out the door and nearly ran into Montana.

"Hey, Sawyer!" Montana backed up a step. "You look like a man on a mission."

"I am. There's a WaveRunner with my name on it out there somewhere."

Montana chuckled. "I take it the zip-lining wasn't your style."

"Not particularly." Though the woman he'd met was. Jenna. Damn, he could kick himself for not asking for her number. Oh, well. He eyed Montana in his swim trunks, T-shirt and flip-flops. "You heading for the beach?"

"I am. Thought I'd improve on my tan." He grinned. "Girls love a tan, right?"

Sawyer turned on the boardwalk path, heading for the ocean. "No date for tonight?"

Montana shook his head. "No. But then, I wasn't really looking."

"Me, either." He hadn't been looking and hadn't made

an attempt when the opportunity bumped into him. He'd be smart to go ahead and ask Quentin to get her number, or he'd spend the rest of the vacation wishing he'd been quicker to seize the moment. "I'm going to rent a Wave-Runner. Wanna go in half?"

"Sure!" Montana flung his towel over his shoulder. "Been a while since I've ridden one."

"Can't imagine the lakes getting warm enough in Montana for a WaveRunner."

"You'd be surprised. We have long days in the summer. Gives the water a chance to warm up."

"From snowmelt?" Sawyer snorted. "Not as warm as the water gets off Virginia Beach."

"Maybe not that warm, but a little warmer than the water off San Diego."

Sawyer shivered. "BUD/S training gave a whole new meaning to word *miserable*."

"Yeah, but I have no regrets."

"Same here." He'd grown up in a wealthy household. Everything he'd wanted, he could have by just asking. BUD/S training had been a real culture shock and an assault on his body, physically and mentally. But he'd be damned if he failed and went home to hear his father say "I told you so."

Everything Sawyer did was to prove to himself he could do anything he set his mind to. Not because his father could get him the position or smooth his way. He didn't want his father's help. Hell, he didn't want anything to do with his father.

The man had given him anything money could buy, but he hadn't been much of a parent. He'd never played ball with him. Never made one of his parent-teacher conferences at school. When Sawyer crashed his motorcycle and broke his arm, his father was in Paris with his fiancée. He didn't bother to come home and check that Sawyer was all right.

He never once showed up at one of his football games. Hell, he didn't *want* him to play football. He'd said the sport was too hard on a man's body. It wrecked the knees. Not that he cared if his son was injured. His advice was from a practical viewpoint. Why destroy your body when you needed it to get you through to old age?

Being raised in a mansion with formal living areas and white carpets had been stifling to Sawyer. He'd never thought he could be himself. He was always the politician's son. On display in his best clothes. Sawyer felt more at ease near the sea, with sand between his toes and the sun warming his skin, wearing nothing but a swimsuit.

"There." Montana pointed down the beach, where a number of WaveRunners rested on the sand. A small tent stood nearby with a menu of prices listed on a chalkboard.

They wove their way between families playing with their children in the sand and bikini-clad beach babes slathered in oil and baking in the sun. Sawyer didn't slow to stare at the beautiful bodies. He wanted to be racing across the water, crashing through the waves, letting the wind and ocean wash thoughts of his lonely childhood from his mind. He had his SEAL brothers now. They were the best family a man could have. They'd be there for him, no matter what.

Sawyer slapped a wad of bills in the attendant's hand. "We'll take one for an hour."

The man pocketed the cash, instructed them on the use of the equipment and helped push a WaveRunner out to the water's edge.

Sawyer nodded to Montana. "You can go first."

"You sure? This was your idea."

"I can wait. Just don't wreck it before I get a chance

to ride." He twisted his lips into a wry grin. "It's not like riding a horse."

Montana laughed, hitched his shorts as if he were a real cowboy dressed in jeans and cowboy boots, and then swung his leg over the seat as if he was mounting a horse. "It's more like riding a horse than you think. But then, riding a horse can be a lot more difficult for you city slickers."

"Keep it up, Montana, and I'll show you a real rodeo on the water."

"Only thing that'll convince me is if you rope a shark, hog-tie him and bring him in to roast on a spit. Montana-style." Montana gunned the throttle and shot out into the water. He hit a small wave head-on, crashing through the crest to emerge on the other side. "Yee-haw!" he yelled and raced out to sea.

Sawyer sat in the wet sand, adjusting the cell phone in his pocket, glad he'd thought to slip it into a waterproof bag before he'd left the bungalow. He let the water lap over his feet and legs, enjoying the sun on his back, the fresh air and the taste of salt on his lips.

The first few days in Cancún had been a lot more than any of them had bargained for. Looking for relaxation, fun and maybe some female companionship, they'd come to Cancún ready for a much-deserved vacation.

Duff had been the first of the men to find a female companion. And boy, did he know how to pick one. Natalie, a former government secret agent, had come to find her sister, who'd disappeared on a diving excursion.

When Duff offered to help, all four members of SEAL Boat Team 22 who'd come to Cancún were engaged to find and liberate women who'd been kidnapped and readied for auction in a human trafficking ring.

Rest and relaxation. Ha!

Since when did getting shot at count as recreation?

Quentin, Montana and Sawyer could have told Duff
where he could go with his plan to help, but that was not
what friends did—not what SEAL brothers did. They stuck
together and helped each other through good times and
bad. And if there were guns and bad guys involved, that
was when they did their best work.

Sawyer leaned back in the surf and let the warm, clear
ocean water ebb and flow over his skin. Now that they'd
retrieved the women and sent most of them to their respec-
tive homes, the team could finish their vacation in peace.

Montana hopped across several more waves, shouting
like a fool and laughing in the sun. A wave hit him broad-
side and knocked the big cowboy into the water.

Laughing, Sawyer stood, brushing sand off his shorts.

Montana dragged himself up the back of the craft,
mounted the WaveRunner and powered into the shore,
pulling up on the sand beside Sawyer. Grinning, he shook
the water from his hair. "You're gonna love it."

"Great."

Montana climbed off and stood to the side.

Finally Sawyer had his turn. He and Montana turned
the vehicle in the sand to aim it outward.

Sawyer swung his leg over the body of the craft and
settled onto the cushioned seat. As he twisted the throttle,
a shout sounded behind him.

As soon as Jenna realized who the man in the photographs
was, she'd grabbed her cell phone and called Carly.

Her friend didn't answer. Instead, she texted.

What do you need? We're in a convertible. I can't hear
over the wind.

Get Quentin to give you the number for his friend.

Carly responded with a smiley face and a note.

His name is Sawyer.

Her heart racing, Jenna paced the floor. Every time she passed the case on the bed, her stomach clenched and she muttered, "Holy crap."

Someone had been paid to deliver Sawyer dead or alive to some undisclosed location. Armed with that information, Jenna couldn't stand by and let the would-be assassin succeed in his mission. She had to warn Sawyer. The sooner the better. The assassin might have more than this rifle at his disposal. And he had a deadline to meet.

Her first thought was to call the police. But no crime had been committed at that point. And hell, what if they thought she was the owner of the weapons? They'd throw her in a Mexican jail to rot. All the reports she'd heard about the Mexican government being owned by the drug cartels didn't give her much faith in their ability to stop this kidnapping or assassination from occurring.

Jenna glanced at the clock on the nightstand. It was already three in the afternoon. That meant six hours until the assassin had to deliver his prize.

Jenna's phone pinged with Carly's text. It contained a phone number, the name of a nearby resort hotel and a message.

Sawyer was planning to go to the beach this afternoon and rent a WaveRunner. You might find him there. Have fun!

"Have fun? Are you kidding me?" With a near-hysterical laugh, Jenna dialed the number and waited, gripping her cell phone so hard, she was afraid she'd break it. On the third ring, a male voice answered.

"Leave a message and I'll get back to you as soon as possible." The voice was the same rich baritone she'd heard on the zip-line platform.

Jenna closed the damning suitcase and shoved it high on a shelf in her closet, hoping that would calm her frazzled nerves. It didn't. She still had to warn Sawyer.

Unwilling to deliver the bad news to him via a recording, she hit the end button and glanced around the room. Still dressed in nothing but her underwear, she yanked the bright pink bikini Carly insisted was adventurous out of her carry-on bag, shed her bra and panties and slipped into the suit. She threw on a short, lacy beach wrap and grabbed her room key.

She'd considered texting Carly about what was in the case but was afraid Carly wouldn't believe her. Or worse, the text message would be intercepted. Nobody could know she had the case. Not until she figured out what to do with it.

First she had to find Sawyer and warn him about the note's contents.

Riding the elevator from the bridal suite to the ground floor was a study in patience. The car stopped several times on the way down to fill with people wearing dinner clothes or beach apparel, depending on where they were headed. They laughed and joked with each other while Jenna bit down on her lip and counted the seconds until they reached the bottom. She wanted to shout and rail at the people slowing her down. Didn't they realize a man's life could be hanging in the balance?

Somewhere in Cancún, possibly on the beach, an assassin could be following Sawyer or aiming at him through a scope similar to the one in the case. One pull of the trigger and Sawyer would be delivered dead.

The elevator hit the ground level and the doors opened, disgorging the numerous passengers.

Dancing in the rear, Jenna tried to get around some of them but was cut off every time. When she found a clear path, she darted through the lobby, making a beeline for the concierge, where she cut in front of an elderly couple and asked where she could find the hotel Carly had given in her text message.

The concierge pointed and told her it was two hotels south along the beach.

Jenna didn't wait for clearer directions but ran out the back door of the hotel, past the pool and the myriad lounge chairs flanking it and out onto the sand. She didn't slow as she raced past the umbrellas and people stretched out, capturing the afternoon sunshine. Eventually she ran along the water's edge, finding better purchase in the wet hard-packed sand. Passing the first resort hotel, she kept her gaze forward, searching the beach in front of her and the water to her left.

God, she hoped he was close to the water, where she could find him easily. If she had to look at each patron on the beach, it could take too much precious time.

As she neared the second resort hotel with its rainbow-colored beach umbrellas, Jenna saw a small tent set up close to the water with a number of WaveRunners parked in the sand.

Barely able to breathe by then, she staggered to a stop in front of the startled attendant.

"Have you—" Jenna wheezed as she leaned against the tent pole and dragged in a deep breath "—rented a Wave-Runner—" she breathed again and finished in a rush "—to a tall, dark-haired man with tattoos on his arms?"

The attendant's brows pulled together. *"Sí."*

"Where is he now?"

The man pointed to the water's edge a hundred yards farther along the beach.

Jenna glanced past the teenagers throwing a Frisbee, the father tossing his child in the air and the girls playing in the surf to a man standing near a WaveRunner and another slinging his leg over the seat.

"Wait!" Jenna cried and took off, running as fast as her legs and lungs could carry her.

Neither man turned at her shout the first time.

"Wait!" she cried as she got closer. This time the man standing beside the WaveRunner looked up. The one on the vehicle revved the engine and started sliding toward the water.

Giving it her all, Jenna lifted her knees and elbows, running faster than she ever had in the fifty-yard dash in high school and pounded across the wet sand, out into the surf. She flung herself onto the back of the watercraft, wrapping her arms around the man with the tattooed arms.

"What the hell?" Sawyer twisted in his seat to stare at his passenger. "Jenna?"

"Go!" she cried. "Go fast! Get as far out as you can."

His gaze sharpened on her face, but he revved the engine. "What's wrong?"

"Just do it. I'll explain when you get away from the shore."

"Are you serious?"

"Yes," she said, holding on tightly as they sped away from the beach and hit a wave full-on. Water splashed up in her face before she could close her mouth. She swallowed some and choked, spitting salt water.

He slowed. "Are you okay?"

"Please, just go out to sea." She clung to his back, her

arms wrapped tightly around his waist. "Your life depends on it."

"Okay." He shook his head but twisted his hand on the throttle, heading out to sea, taking them farther and farther from the beach.

When they were a good quarter of a mile out, he slowed the vehicle to a stop and half turned to face her. "Now, do you mind telling me what the hell just happened?"

Jenna glanced back at the shore. "How far can a bullet travel?"

"What?" Sawyer stared at her as if she'd lost her mind. "Not that I'm not flattered, but what does that have to do with hijacking me and my WaveRunner?"

She wiped the salty water from her face and bit her lip. "You're not going to believe this." Shaking her head, she tried to pull the words together in her mind before blurting them out.

"Believe what?" His scowl deepened. "Woman, you aren't making sense. And if you don't start talking, I'm heading back to shore before we run out of gas or the engine decides to quit. I'm pretty sure we're farther out than the attendant recommended."

Jenna's heart thumped against her chest and her fingers dug into his waist. "Someone is going to try to kill you."

For a long moment he stared down at her. "Is that your prediction? Are you a psychic or something?" His lips curled in a derisive smile. "Lady, I'm a SEAL. I get shot at on every mission."

Jenna shook her head. "How can you believe me when I barely believe what I saw?" She pressed her forehead to his shoulder, grasping for the words. Then she straightened, firming her jaw. "I picked up the wrong suitcase in the lobby of my hotel. When I opened it, I found what I assume were the parts to assemble a sniper's rifle, complete with a scope."

Sawyer snorted. "How do *you* know what a sniper's rifle looks like? Do you even own a gun?"

Her cheeks heated, and anger spiked inside her. "So, I don't own a gun, and I don't know exactly what a sniper's rifle looks like. But it's what was with the rifle that made me assume the owner was a sniper, hit man or assassin."

With a chuckle, Sawyer ran a hand through his dark, wet hair, standing it on end. "Could it be you've been watching or reading too many thrillers lately?"

She smacked her palm against his arm. "Damn it, I'm trying to tell you that I found photographs and a note with the weapon. Your photographs. Pictures of you and a note telling the gun owner to bring you to wherever they were going to meet by nine o'clock tonight. Dead or alive."

This time Sawyer sat still, his gaze pinning hers.

Jenna held steady, lifting her chin.

"How do I know you're not some nutcase desperate for male companionship and will come up with any cockamamie story to get one alone?"

Jenna let go of his waist and scooted back on the seat of the WaveRunner. "Is that what you think?" She slipped even farther back until she teetered on the edge, refusing to touch even one inch of the man's body. "Do you think I'm so desperate I'd chase a man out into the middle of the ocean just to get him alone?" She shook her head. "You know, I could have taken that case to hotel security and let them handle it."

"Why didn't you?"

"It doesn't matter. It's your life on the line. Not mine. If you want to ignore the warning I've given you out of the sincerest desire to save your sorry carcass, you do that. I'll just get myself back to shore, because I'd rather swim a mile in shark-infested waters than ride back on a Wave-Runner operated by a man with an ego the size of a whale." She dived into the water before he could say anything or reach out and grab her.

Jenna struck out, headed for shore, weighed down by her beach wrap. She hadn't done much swimming since she'd been on the high school swim team, and she realized almost immediately that she didn't have the strength she once had. But sheer anger should fuel her long enough to make it back to shore.

She sure as hell wasn't going to ride with an arrogant, self-centered, stupid man who could be dead by morning because he thought she was a desperate crackpot.

The WaveRunner engine fired up behind her.

Jenna continued to swim freestyle, trying to remember how to time her breathing and making smooth, steady strokes, pacing herself so that she wouldn't get too tired too quickly.

Sawyer pulled up beside her. "Get on."

She ignored him, choosing to breathe rather than waste her strength arguing.

Damn the man, but he kept pace with her, bobbing beside her on the water craft.

"I'm sorry," Sawyer said. "I shouldn't have called you a desperate nutcase."

It was a start, but he had a long way to go before she forgave him for saying all those nasty things to her. Jenna plowed through the buoyant salt water, one stroke at a time, refusing to acknowledge the man.

He sped up, pulling ahead of her.

Fine. Go back to shore.

Jenna would make it on her own. She didn't need a man to rescue her. The men in her life hadn't proven to be very reliable. Or at least her ex-fiancé hadn't. Sawyer, though not really a part of her life, wasn't much better. She'd done him a favor. Tried to save his sorry life. And what did she get in return? Grief. To hell with him. He could be shot for all she cared.

A splash ahead made her stop and tread water.

The WaveRunner seat was empty, and Sawyer was nowhere to be seen.

Chapter Three

Jenna's pulse jumped and she spun in a circle, searching for him.

Had the assassin gunned him down?

She looked for the telltale sign of blood mixing with the ocean water but couldn't see any. Dragging in a deep breath, she dived beneath the surface in search of Sawyer's body.

Salt water stung her eyes before she'd swum four feet toward the WaveRunner. Jenna surfaced, blinking.

The water erupted, and Sawyer's face appeared in front of her.

Jenna started to scream, inhaled a gulp of ocean and coughed until tears streamed from her eyes and she sank below the water.

A strong arm wrapped around her middle and dragged her to the surface. "Are you all right?" Sawyer spun her to face him and pushed the sodden hanks of hair from her face.

"I thought you were dead," she said, her voice hoarse from coughing.

He shook his head. "I'm okay. It's you I was worried about. It's too far for you to swim back, and there might be a riptide. I couldn't let you do it."

She drew in a steadying breath and glared at him. "You could have been shot."

"Yeah, well, I wasn't."

"But you could have been." She wiped tears from her eyes, pushed at his chest and swam away from him, using a breaststroke.

"I'm really sorry I didn't take you seriously," Sawyer said, easily keeping pace.

Jenna nodded toward the watercraft, drifting farther and farther away from them. "You better go catch your ride before you lose it, too."

"I'm not going to leave you out here. If I have to let the WaveRunner go, I will." He stuck with her.

Jenna's conscience couldn't let him sacrifice an expensive machine for her. Besides, she was wasting time. The expense was the least of his worries. She stopped swimming and trod water. "Okay. But we need to bring it in at a different location. If you know you have a sniper gunning for you, you can't just present yourself as a target. I would have presumed they'd taught you that in SEAL training."

Sawyer chuckled. "They did. I promise to bring it in to a different location." He didn't make a move. "Are you coming with me?"

She glanced at the shore, admitting to herself, even if not aloud, that it was farther than she really had the strength or stamina to achieve. "Yes."

"Can you make it to the WaveRunner? Or do you want to wait here and let me come back and pick you up?"

"I can swim," she said, refusing to show any weakness to this man.

"Okay, then." He struck out.

Jenna followed, barely able to keep up with his stronger strokes. By the time she reached the WaveRunner, Sawyer had climbed aboard and revved the engine.

When he reached out a hand, she took it.

With very little effort, he pulled her out of the water, and she settled on the machine behind him. Her arms aching, she wrapped them around his waist and held on while he set the watercraft on a path toward the shore, but not toward the resort where he'd entered the water. He aimed toward her resort hotel.

"I'm not sure this is a good idea, either. Apparently the gunman is staying at this hotel."

"Well, where would you have me stop?"

She sighed. "You might as well stop here. You need to see for yourself what I'm talking about. But you can't stand still long. He could be targeting you as we speak."

Sawyer pulled up on the sand and shut off the engine.

"We'd better get inside. It's not safe to be out in the open." Jenna glanced at the sun starting its descent toward the horizon. "There are only a few hours until nine o'clock. If the gunman wants to make his deadline, he'll be coming after you."

Jenna scanned the beach, searching beneath the umbrellas. Then she faced the multistoried hotels, looking for anyone positioned on a balcony, aiming a rifle at Sawyer.

"You'll have to come to my hotel room. I can show you the case, the gun and the note. Hell, you can have them, for that matter. I don't want the Mexican police to catch me in possession of a weapon."

Sawyer frowned. "You say you mistook the case for yours. Where exactly is your case now?"

Jenna shook her head. "It was supposed to arrive by the time I got back from zip-lining. That's why I grabbed the one I found."

"If you mistook the case with the gun for yours—" Sawyer's jaw tightened "—is it possible the gunman took your case instead?"

Jenna nodded. "I suppose it's possible." She grabbed his arm and started toward the hotel. "The main thing right now is to get you out of rifle range." She marched ahead, holding on to his arm until he brought her to an abrupt stop. Jenna faced him. "Do you have a death wish?"

Sawyer shook his head. "Sweetheart, you realize that if this man finds out he has the wrong case, he'll come looking for the right one."

"Yeah. So?"

"Did you leave any identification on or inside your case?"

"Of course. How else was the airline going to know who it belonged to?" Jenna bit her lip, dread filling her belly. She'd been so concerned about warning Sawyer, she hadn't thought about herself.

Sawyer's glance shot left, right and forward as if he now was searching for the gunman. "You could be in as much danger as I'm supposed to be, if that gunman finds out where you're staying."

"Then we'd better get back to my room before he finds his case."

Sawyer shook his head. "I'm not so sure that's a good idea, either. He could already be there."

Jenna's heart slipped to the pit of her belly. "We have to get there. Fast."

"Why?"

"I have a roommate."

"Isn't she the one Quentin is with right now?"

"Yes. But I don't know when she'll be back." Jenna walked with purpose toward the hotel, digging her bare feet into the sand. Should the gunman come looking for his case… Holy hell…

Sawyer kept pace.

Jenna shot a glance toward Sawyer. "Shouldn't you be ducking your head or hiding your face?"

"I'll grab a hat in the hotel's gift shop on the way back to my hotel." He held out his hand. "First let's get that case. Give me your key. I'll check your room."

She dug the key out of her wrap pocket, amazed it hadn't floated out when she'd gone swimming. Slapping it into his palm, she stepped into the elevator.

Sawyer entered behind her, his finger hovering over the keypad. "What floor?"

"The top," she said and cringed. The last thing she wanted to tell Sawyer was that she was staying in the bridal suite. Hell, he'd find out soon enough.

As the elevator rose, Sawyer pulled a cell phone out of a waterproof bag.

"I doubt the police will be of much help," Jenna commented.

"I'm not calling the police. I'm texting my friend I left back on the beach to let him know where I left the Wave-Runner." He finished his text and hit Send.

When the elevator stopped at the top floor, Sawyer held out a hand, stopping Jenna from exiting. "Wait until I clear the hallway."

"My room's at the end." Jenna stood back, holding her finger on the door-open button while Sawyer disappeared down the corridor.

With her breath lodged in her throat, Jenna waited for Sawyer's signal.

It wasn't long before his voice echoed down the hallway. "What the hell?"

SAWYER HAD MADE a sweep of the hallway, checked the stairwell and tried the handles on the doors to the other penthouse suites. Each door had a fancy black placard with gold lettering naming the suite. When he'd come to the end of the corridor, he stopped and took a step backward.

"Seriously? You're staying in the bridal suite?"

Jenna left the safety of the elevator and joined him in front of the door. "It's a long story."

"I'd love to hear it sometime." He slid the key over the lock, and the light blinked green. "Soon." Sawyer opened the door. "In the meantime, stay here."

Again, he went ahead of her, stepping into the spacious living area with floor-to-ceiling windows overlooking the ocean. With the sun angling toward the horizon, the beach-goers had thinned, leaving a few couples walking hand in hand along the shoreline.

He didn't spend much time checking out the scenery. He was more concerned about who else might be occupying the room. Still not convinced he or Jenna had anything to worry about, he made a thorough sweep of the living area, bedroom, closets and bathroom. "All clear," he called out and turned to find Jenna standing in the doorway of the bathroom. "You were supposed to wait."

"Sorry. I can be impatient. It's one of my flaws. Along with being boring." She left the doorway and crossed to the closet.

Sawyer followed. "I can see the impatience, but you don't really believe you're boring, do you?"

Jenna shrugged, her lips pressing into a thin line, her cheeks turning a light shade of pink. "I don't know what to think about myself. I suppose I am boring."

Clenching his fists, Sawyer wished he could punch the person who'd fed Jenna that line of bull. "You're repeating what your ex-fiancé said."

"In so many words." She slid the door back to reveal a gray hard-sided suitcase wedged onto the top shelf. Jenna pointed to it. "That's it. Proof I'm not a desperate female after your gorgeous body to save me from dying alone."

He touched her arm.

She flinched away.

He wished he could take back what he'd said to her. He didn't need to add to her self-esteem issues. She had enough of those already. And as far as he could tell, she had no reason for them. With her long, dark ginger curls and bright green eyes, she was practically perfect, except for the frown denting her forehead. Sawyer wanted to brush his thumb across the lines. "I said I was sorry." He gave her a crooked smile. "You don't let things go, do you?"

"Add that to my list of faults." She backed away and let Sawyer pull the case off the shelf.

He carried it across to the bed and set it down. "I'll add that to your list of positive attributes. If this case holds what you say it does, I'm lucky that you don't give up easily." He flicked the catches, and the case remained locked.

Jenna handed him a metal file. "Use this."

She was not only beautiful, and anything but boring, but also smart and resourceful. He jammed the file into the locks and flipped them open one at a time.

Inside were neatly folded shirts and trousers. As he peered closer, he noticed the inside of the case wasn't as deep as the exterior indicated. He set the clothes to the side and looked again.

With a huff of impatience, Jenna reached around him and ran her finger along the inside. A partition popped up.

As he lifted the divider, his gut clenched. Just as Jenna had said, there were parts that would make a complete sniper's rifle with a military-grade scope, giving the shooter the capability of firing at long distances.

"This is what made me find you." Jenna lifted the envelope and turned it upside down, shaking the contents out onto the bed.

Photographs of Sawyer fanned out on the comforter. Pictures of him walking on the streets of New Orleans when he'd spent a weekend there with his teammates, shots of him outside his apartment near Stennis in Mississippi, and even more of him when he'd last visited his father in DC three months ago. Whoever had been following him had been doing so for some time.

"I don't understand." He shook his head. "Why me?"

"Darlin', if you don't know—" Jenna let out a short, hard laugh "—I can't help you. Have you pissed off someone in your past? Someone who would want revenge?"

He thought back on the missions he'd been a part of. The most recent sanctioned mission had to do with a terrorist training camp in Honduras. Surely the terrorists involved hadn't come all the way to Cancún and singled him out. Why not the rest of his team? He shuffled through the photographs.

Whoever the assassin was, Sawyer was his only target.

Sawyer drew in a deep breath and let it out, then glanced across at Jenna. "My father is a US senator. Not many people know, but this doesn't make sense. The note doesn't make sense."

Jenna read it aloud. "'Bring him to the agreed-upon location by 9:00 p.m. Dead or alive.'" She stared at the paper, her face pale, her eyes wide. "I don't know. Why would someone kill you and then deliver you somewhere?"

"Unless they're trying to make a statement."

Her pretty brow furrowed. "What kind of statement?"

"Perhaps it's a drug cartel or terrorist organization picking off SEALs to show they can." He shoved a hand through his hair. "Whoever it is hired an assassin. He might get paid more if he delivers me alive."

"Or he might just decide to take a lesser payoff because he's dealing with a highly trained SEAL. If he can pick you off at a distance, he has less of a chance of being taken down."

Sawyer's lips quirked. "You're pretty smart." He cupped her cheek and stared into her beautiful green eyes, wanting to do so much more. When he finally looked away, he dropped his hands to his sides. Settling the photos and note into the case, he closed it and let the locks click into place. Then he stared around the room as if for the first time. "Why the bridal suite?"

She turned and walked toward the floor-to-ceiling windows. "It's a dumb story."

"I still want to hear it." He followed and stood behind her, watching her instead of the view. He liked what he saw: petite, yet strong; slim, yet curvy; smart and a bit sassy.

"I was engaged to a man who found my maid of honor more interesting than me." She shrugged. "He texted me on our wedding day that he couldn't go through with the marriage." She turned and waved her hand at the room. "The hotel was nonrefundable, so I came with a friend." She lifted her chin and faced him, her eyes slightly narrowed as if daring him to laugh.

Again, he cupped her face. "His loss, my gain. If you'd come with him, you might not have found the case and come to warn me." He lifted her hand and pressed a kiss to the backs of her knuckles. "Thank you. And for the record, your fiancé was a fool."

"Ex-fiancé," she amended, staring at the hand he kissed. "And I agree. I'm better off without him." She stood as if frozen to the spot, her eyes widening as her tongue swept across pale pink lips.

Sawyer couldn't resist. He bent to brush his mouth

across hers in what he'd intended as a brief sweep. But as soon as his lips connected with hers, he couldn't back away. He slipped his hands around her waist and pulled her close, deepening the kiss.

She rested her palms on his chest. Instead of pushing him away, her fingers curled into him, her nails scraping against his skin.

He skimmed the seam of her lips, and she opened to him.

He caressed her tongue with his, fire burning through his veins, searing a path south to his groin.

Jenna's hands slid up his chest and linked behind his neck, pulling him closer.

The sound of a metal lock clicking brought Sawyer out of the trance Jenna's mouth had him in, and he lifted his head.

"Oh." The woman who'd been with Jenna at the zip line stopped in the middle of the doorway, her eyes rounding. "I'm sorry. I didn't mean to disturb you." She pointed to the closet and hurried across the room. "I'll just be a minute," she said, tiptoeing into the room, grimacing. "Don't mind me. Go back to what you were doing." She grabbed a dress and raced into the bathroom, calling out over her shoulder, "I didn't see anything. Continue kissing."

Jenna stepped away from Sawyer, her cheeks bright red, her eyes averted. She pressed a hand to her lips and stared out the window.

When the bathroom door opened again, her friend smiled. "Don't wait up for me. I might not be back. I'm taking my toothbrush just in case." She rushed to the door, yanked it open and turned with a full grin on her face. "And for the record, Tyler didn't deserve you. And you deserve to have fun. You go, girl!" She pumped her fist and let the door close automatically behind her.

"Don't mind Carly. She has no filter." Jenna chuckled softly. "She'd tell you that herself."

"I get that."

"Should we catch her before she gets on the elevator and warn her about the hit man?" Jenna started for the door.

"No. Text her and tell her you'd like to have the room to yourself. That should keep her from coming back to a potentially dangerous situation."

Jenna texted the message.

Carly texted back with a smiley face.

God, she probably thought Sawyer was staying the night. Jenna's cheeks heated and she couldn't face the man. Instead, she walked back toward the gunman's bag. "What do I do with the case? Should I take it back to the lobby and leave it for its owner?"

"No use making it easy for him to kill me. If he wants me badly enough, he'll have to find another weapon to do the job."

Jenna shivered. "I'd just as soon he didn't do the job at all."

"You and me both."

"In the meantime, what do I do with it?" Jenna waved at the case.

"I'll take it. I know someone who might help." He lifted the suitcase off the bed and headed for the door.

Jenna jumped in front of him. "Wait a minute. Where are you going?"

"Back to my room."

"If he knows you're in Cancún, the assassin will know which room you're in." She touched his arm. "You can't go back there."

"What do you suggest?"

She glanced around the bridal suite. "I figure if he

hasn't already come after me for the case, chances are he doesn't know I have it."

"Then this will have to stay here for now." Sawyer hefted the gun case onto the shelf in the closet and straightened, facing Jenna. "We need to find your case before he does."

"Right." Jenna nodded. "I guess you can stay here until I get back. I hope my case has been delivered from the airport by now."

"Uh-uh." Sawyer shook his head. "You're not going anywhere without me."

Her brows pulled together. "But he'll recognize you as soon as you set foot into the lobby—if he didn't see you coming in the first time."

"Not if I wear a hat and sunglasses." He glanced around the room. "I don't suppose you have a T-shirt that will fit me and a baseball cap or sunglasses." He stared down at his naked chest. "I seem to have come ill-prepared for undercover ops. If not, I'll pick up something in the gift shop."

Jenna's gaze zeroed in on his chest, and as they had so often in the past few minutes, her cheeks flamed. "I might have something," she said and hurried toward the dresser. After riffling through her clothes for a few seconds, she surfaced with an oversize black, white and gold New Orleans Saints football jersey.

Sawyer held it up. "Are you a fan?"

"I am." She lifted her chin. "And damn proud of it. So don't talk bad about my Saints."

He winked and dragged the jersey over his head and shoulders. "I wouldn't dream of it. But isn't the shirt a little big for you?"

"It's perfect to sleep in," she said, her cheeks reddening again. She handed him a pair of mirrored sunglasses and a Saints ball cap. "Ready?"

He slipped the glasses onto his face and the cap on his head and nodded. "Let's go. But me first."

Jenna frowned. "Do you think he might be on the other side of the door?" She stepped in front of him. "Maybe I should go first."

"Lady, you're killing my ego." He smoothed his hand behind her head, grabbed those lush red curls and tugged, tilting her head back. "But you're beautiful when you do it." Sawyer kissed her hard on the lips, set her away from the door and reached for the handle.

Chapter Four

Jenna bunched her fists. If the assassin waited on the other side of the door, it would take only one bullet to kill Sawyer.

"Stand back." With one hand on the door, Sawyer pushed Jenna out of sight. He glanced through the peephole and then stood to the side as he eased open the door. "Stay."

"I'm not a dog," she muttered, her breath catching and holding as Sawyer peered into the hallway and then stepped out. "I'll be right back." He left her in the room, the door automatically closing between them.

Jenna ran to the peephole and peered through. She could see only straight across the hallway to a blank wall. No Sawyer.

She gripped the door handle and remembered Sawyer's order. Instead of opening the door, she made herself count to ten. If Sawyer wasn't back by then, she'd go looking for him.

At nine, a light knock sounded on the door.

Jenna glanced through the peephole and then jerked open the door, flinging herself into Sawyer's arms.

"Hey." He chuckled. "I was only gone three seconds."

"Eight," she said, peeling herself off him, feeling foolish for being so dramatic. "But who's counting?"

"The hallway and the stairwell are clear. Let's go." He took her hand and drew it through his arm, bringing her body close to his.

She liked being against him. Something about Sawyer made her feel protected and safe in this new world of danger and intrigue in which she'd landed. Who would have thought mild-mannered, boring Jenna would end up embroiled in an assassin's plot to murder a navy SEAL?

Well, she'd wanted to break out of her normal routine. This was as far from normal as she could have imagined.

They walked arm in arm down the corridor.

A doorway opened across from the elevator.

Sawyer stepped forward, putting his body in front of hers.

Jenna's heart squeezed hard in her chest. Tyler hadn't done anything to protect her. Not even hold an umbrella over her head in the rain. And hell, she'd never been in a situation where bullets were involved, but she was pretty certain Tyler wouldn't have stepped between her and a potential shooter.

Jenna's knees shook as she peered around Sawyer, praying he wasn't about to be shot.

A young couple dressed in semiformal clothes spilled out of the room, laughing and holding each other like newlyweds. They walked straight across the hallway and hit the button on the elevator to go down.

By the time Jenna and Sawyer reached the elevator, the bell dinged and the door slid open.

Again Jenna had a moment of panic, expecting a gunman to spring from inside, wielding a machine gun, mowing down anything that moved. Her hand tightened on Sawyer's arm.

He covered it with his own. "It's empty," he whispered, leading her in next to the clingy couple.

"Are you the newlyweds from the bridal suite?" the woman asked, practically wearing her man.

Jenna's cheeks heated and she opened her mouth to stammer a denial, but Sawyer beat her to it.

"Yes, we are." He slipped his arm around Jenna's waist and pulled her snugly against his side. "Aren't we, sweetheart?" He bent to kiss her.

Taken off guard, Jenna couldn't think of a response and was saved from having to by the brush of his lips across hers.

"Umm," he said, deepening the kiss.

Jenna's pulse quickened.

"We tried to get the bridal suite, but it was booked when we made our reservations," the woman said. "Not that I'm complaining. They assured us our room had most of the same accoutrements, minus the hot tub for two." She pouted and stared into her new husband's eyes. "We'll have to come back on our one-year anniversary, won't we?"

Her husband winked and bent to nuzzle her neck. "Maybe we'll just stay here forever."

She giggled, and the bell rang announcing their arrival at the lobby level.

The door slid open, and Sawyer tensed against Jenna.

Before Jenna and Sawyer could move, the gushingly happy newlyweds stepped out. "Congrats on your wedding," the bride said, her eyes sparkling, a smile splitting her face. Blissfully unaware of potential danger lurking around every corner.

"Congrats to you," Jenna called out. That was supposed to be her on this trip. Happily married to Tyler, giggling and clinging to him.

Then Jenna realized that would never have been her. She and Tyler had never been openly demonstrative, preferring to kiss in private. Or had that been mostly on Tyler's part?

Jenna frowned.

Sawyer had kissed her in front of the other couple, something Tyler would never have done willingly. Then again, Sawyer had been playing the part of the newlywed who couldn't keep from kissing his bride.

Jenna bet he wouldn't be a prude about open displays of affection with the woman he loved. Which made her think. "By the way, are you married?" she whispered.

Sawyer had taken a step out of the elevator into the lobby. He ground to a stop, and the elevator nearly closed before Jenna could get out.

At the last second, he grabbed her hand and tugged, dragging her through the door and into his arms. He bent to kiss her firmly on the mouth and then trailed a line of kisses up to her earlobe. "I might not be the best boyfriend material," he whispered into her ear.

His warm breath sent shivers of awareness throughout her body.

"But I wouldn't kiss another woman if I were married." He kissed her again on the mouth. "Satisfied?"

Satisfied? Hardly. One kiss didn't seem to be enough with this man. She might never be satisfied. If it had been a different situation, she might demand more kisses to see if she finally grew tired of them.

She couldn't imagine that ever happening.

Sawyer straightened and glanced around behind the relative anonymity of the mirrored sunglasses and ball cap.

Meanwhile, Jenna's body trembled. She feared she might have melted into the floor if Sawyer hadn't been holding her around the waist.

"We should check with the concierge to see if your bag has arrived from the airport," Sawyer said.

"Yes. My bag." Jenna's cheeks burned. Did she sound

that airheaded? The SEAL's kisses made her forget everything, including the fact that a gunman was after him.

An image of the sniper-rifle parts flashed through her mind, bringing her back to reality. Sawyer was in danger. She needed to focus on him and keeping him safe.

"Over here." Jenna led him toward the registration counter. To the side of the long counter was the concierge's desk. Jenna couldn't help but stare at every man they passed and wonder if he was the assassin.

The gray-haired man with the handlebar mustache could be an undercover assassin. Who would suspect an older guy? And the mustache would make it hard to run facial-recognition software on him. He could be a highly experienced assassin with a long list of kills in his lifetime.

The man in the khaki slacks and pale blue polo shirt could be a master at blending in. Was he staring at them? Jenna tried not to stare back, watching him from the corner of her eye until they'd passed him. A shiver of awareness trickled down her back. Was he the one?

Intent on studying the man in the blue polo shirt, Jenna bumped into someone else. "Pardon me," she said and scooted out of the way of a man with light brown hair and gray eyes. He wore jeans and a gray T-shirt and seemed slightly familiar, but not in a distinct way—more as if she'd seen a hundred similar guys before.

Her gaze shifted to the sandy-blond-haired gentleman wearing jeans, a button-up white shirt and cowboy boots. He could have learned to fire expertly on a ranch in west Texas. Jenna's imagination concocted all sorts of scenarios, and she didn't see the woman until she ran into her hard enough to knock her own purse out of her hand.

"I'm so sorry," the woman said. "I can be pretty clumsy." She dropped to her haunches to help Jenna retrieve the contents of her purse.

Jenna bent to gather a pen, a tube of lipstick and her luggage receipts. "No, it was my fault. I should watch where I'm going." When she straightened, she smiled at the woman with the long dark hair pulled back in a neat, stylish ponytail.

She wore a tailored pantsuit in a soft cream color with a pale blue blouse beneath. "Are you sure you're okay?"

"I am." Jenna slipped her purse strap over her shoulder.

"Whew. I didn't want to start my vacation off causing an injury. I hope you enjoy Cancún. I plan on it." She smiled and walked away, stopping at a brochure stand near the excursion planner's table.

Sawyer cupped her elbow and led her toward the concierge's desk.

A man stood behind it, talking on a house phone. When they approached, he ended his call and set the handset on the base. "How can I help you?"

Jenna stepped forward. "My suitcase didn't arrive with me, and the airline assured me it would be sent on as soon as they found it. I don't suppose it's shown up?"

The concierge clicked on a computer keyboard, his head bent, his eyes skimming the screen. Then he glanced up. "We had a delivery over an hour ago, and I believe that's another arriving right now." He nodded toward the door. "Do you have your claim ticket?"

She handed the claim ticket to the concierge and waited while he checked in a room behind him, coming out empty-handed. "It's not in the storage room, but let me check with the bellboy bringing in the latest arrivals' luggage."

Before he finished speaking, a bellboy wheeled in a cart loaded with luggage. On top was a case just like the one back in the bridal suite with a sniper's rifle inside. "That might be the one. The hard-sided gray one with the chrome grip." Jenna pointed to the case.

The bellboy grabbed it from the top and handed it to the concierge, who held the claim ticket up to the strip of paper looped around the handle and smiled. "This is your bag."

Jenna resisted the urge to snatch the case and run. Instead, she smiled and handed the bellboy a tip. "Thank you." With as much dignity as she could muster, she turned toward the elevator and walked, though her feet wanted to fly.

The elevator was already crowded, but several others entered the elevator with her and Sawyer. The man in the cowboy boots and the one with the blue polo shirt stepped into the car right before the doors closed. As more people crowded in, Jenna bumped into someone behind her.

A feminine chuckle sounded. "We have to stop meeting this way."

Jenna turned in the tight space to find the brunette standing against the back of the elevator car.

"We're bound to since we're in the same hotel." The woman held out a hand. "Hi. I'm Becca Smith."

Jenna took her hand. "Jenna Broyles."

Becca eyed Sawyer. Jenna opened her mouth to introduce him, but he beat her to it.

"I'm Mr. Broyles, Jenna's husband." His lips turned up at the corners, causing her heart to flip. "We're still trying to get used to the fact we're married now."

Becca's brows rose. "Oh, newlyweds." She glanced at Jenna's hand. "Show me your ring. I'll bet it's gorgeous."

Heat crawled up Jenna's neck, and she hid her hand behind her back.

Sawyer's arm slipped around her waist and pulled her close. "She had to leave it at the jeweler's. One of the prongs holding in a diamond came loose."

"Yes," Jenna said, relief making her gush a little too

much. "I didn't want to lose a diamond on the trip. I thought it best to have it taken care of while I was gone."

"Good thinking," Becca said. She nodded toward the suitcase. "Only one suitcase between the two of you?"

Jenna laughed. "Hardly. This one was late."

The elevator slid to a stop on the third floor, and the man in the blue polo shirt got off without having spoken a word or glancing in their direction the entire ride up.

One fewer suspect in the car with them didn't make Jenna any more relaxed.

Becca glanced down at the brochures in her hands. "Are you two planning any excursions? I was thinking of deep-sea fishing, parasailing or zip-lining."

"I don't know about the fishing or parasailing," Jenna responded. "But the zip-lining was okay."

Sawyer snorted. "If you don't mind heights and plunging hundreds of feet down a cliff into the dark jungle."

The brunette looked from Jenna to Sawyer and back. "I take it you two went and didn't enjoy it?"

Jenna shrugged. "The anticipation of a violent death was worse than the actual event."

"You have no idea," Sawyer muttered.

The bell dinged and Becca said, "This is my floor. I hope to bump into you again." She edged her way through several others and exited.

The man in the cowboy boots got off on the next floor, stopped and turned back toward the elevator doors as they closed. He stared into the car, his eyes narrowing. Jenna could swear he was looking straight at her.

A shiver shook her frame as the elevator rose. People got out until she and Sawyer were the only two left to ride the rest of the way to the top floor.

Jenna held her comments until they stood outside the bridal suite. "I'm getting twitchy."

Sawyer ran the key card over the reader. The green light flashed on, and he pushed the door open. "What do you mean?" he asked, holding the door for Jenna to enter.

He followed, letting go of the door. It closed, shutting them into the room, away from prying eyes and curious people. Once inside, he pulled off the cap and sunglasses, exposing his gorgeous dark brown eyes and rumpled brown hair.

Off balance because of his mere presence, Jenna put distance between them. "I couldn't read the people in the lobby." She crossed the large living area and ducked into the bedroom.

"What people were you trying to read?" Sawyer followed her, stopping in the doorway, his arms crossed over his chest.

Jenna hefted her suitcase onto the bed and flicked open the clasps. With a sense of relief, she stared down at the beautiful clothes she'd purchased with Carly's help before the trip. For the past year, she'd scrimped and saved for the wedding and the honeymoon. And for what? Her groom ran off with her former best friend. Fortunately, they hadn't combined their bank accounts, or she might have been out all of her savings.

She'd taken half the money they would have used for a down payment on a house and bought a whole new wardrobe, including sexy lingerie, with the intention of having the time of her life…and maybe even a fling while in Cancún…without Tyler.

She glanced from beneath her lashes at the man in the doorway, her imagination running rampant. A fling with Sawyer would far exceed her expectations. He was infinitely more muscular than Tyler, besides being utterly sexy and dangerous. Her heart fluttered, and she had to bring herself back to what was important. The danger that surrounded them.

"What bothered me most about going to the lobby and even riding up in a crowded elevator was the unknown," Jenna said. "The assassin could have been any one of the people in the lobby or elevator. He might appear to be a man on vacation in khaki slacks…"

"Or a guy in a blue polo shirt," Sawyer finished for her.

She nodded. "You were looking, too, weren't you?"

He straightened. "Now that you have your suitcase, you might be in the clear. All the more reason for me to get the gun case out of your possession."

Jenna gnawed on her lower lip. "What are you going to do with it?"

"I know someone who could run fingerprints on it."

"Haven't we handled it too much to lift clean prints?" she asked. What was she saying? She knew nothing about fingerprints and how to collect them.

"Did you pick up the rifle?" Sawyer asked.

"No."

"Neither did I. We might be able to lift prints from the stock or scope."

"Well, let's get it to your guy." She closed her suitcase and started for the closet where she'd stored the gun case.

Sawyer stepped in front of her, his eyes narrowed as if thinking. "I'd have to go back by my bungalow to deliver the case."

Jenna's pulse sped. "You can't." She stopped in front of him. "If the gunman knows you're here in Cancún, he'll know where to look for you. The hotel you checked into. You can't get near the bungalow. That would be giving him an easy target."

Sawyer's lips curled upward, making Jenna's insides quiver. "Unlike being on a WaveRunner jetting out to sea?"

She frowned. "At least I got your attention, as well as getting you out of range of a sniper's rifle."

"Which he didn't have because you pilfered it, mistaking it for your own case."

Jenna sighed and looked up at him. "What if I hadn't mistaken the case? You never would have known someone was after you until it was too late."

He took her hand and drew her closer. "In case I haven't told you already…thanks for saving my life."

Jenna stared down at his hand holding hers. "Anyone would have done it."

"No. Not anyone. You might have taken the case straight to the police."

She glanced up. "I did consider them, but concluded they might not understand the case isn't mine. They might have thrown me in jail rather than help you. You were in more immediate danger, and a visit from the Cancún police would have slowed me down."

Sawyer lifted her hand to his lips. "Thank you again for risking your life to save mine."

Jenna's gaze was captured by Sawyer's, and she fell into his dark brown gaze. "You're wel—"

He covered her mouth with his. His hands dropped to her waist, pulling her hips against his. The hard evidence of his desire pressed against her belly.

Jenna moaned and opened to him.

Sawyer slid his tongue between her teeth and she met him, her tongue twisting and turning in a dance of desire. When at last Sawyer raised his head, Jenna swayed, bracing her hands on his chest. "You have to stop doing that."

"Why?"

"I barely know you."

"You knew enough about me to find me on the beach

and save me from an assassin. I reckon that gives us a pass on convention."

She rested her forehead against his chest. "I didn't come to Cancún to get involved with a man." But, boy, had that backfired on her.

He sighed. "And I have no business getting involved with you." He gripped her shoulders and set her at arm's length. "As a SEAL, I'm gone more than I'm home. And with an assassin after me, I can't risk you becoming collateral damage."

Jenna stared up at him, narrowing her eyes. "What do you mean?"

His jaw tightened. "Since you found your case, we can probably assume the gunman didn't mistake it for his. He can't know you have his gun. You're in the clear."

"So?"

"If you're in the clear, I need to step away so you aren't caught in the cross fire if things go bad. I don't want anyone connecting the dots between us."

What he was saying slowly sank in, and Jenna stepped back, out of his grip. "Does this mean you'll take it from here? I'm not needed anymore?"

He nodded. "That's exactly what I mean. As long as someone is after me, I'm a target. Anyone who gets close to me becomes a target, as well." He walked to the closet and pulled down the case. "Once I leave this hotel, I'll ditch the hat and glasses and resume my existence as Sawyer Houston."

"The walking target." Jenna shook her head. "That's crazy. You should hide. The assassin might have a backup rifle pointed at your bungalow, just waiting for you to return."

"Or he's scrambling to find a new one." Sawyer faced her, the case in his hand. "You don't happen to have a laundry bag or beach bag big enough to disguise the case, do you?"

Jenna stood motionless, her mind racing, her thoughts focused on Sawyer. "I have a beach bag," she said and moved toward her other suitcase with the giant folding beach bag she'd packed to carry her beach towel, hat and sunscreen. It was big enough to carry the small gray suitcase with not much room to spare. As she pulled the beach bag out of her luggage, she faced him. "So, you're just going to walk out of here and not let me help anymore?"

He took the beach bag from her and nodded. "That's right. I couldn't live with myself if something happened to you because of me."

Jenna propped a fist on her hip and squared off with him. "Don't you think that's my choice?"

He shook his head. "Not when it could cost you your life." He stuffed the case into the oversize bag and tied the handles together. "You shouldn't be seen with me, especially if I'm not wearing the disguise."

"I'll take my chances."

"Okay, I don't want you to follow me around."

Her mouth firmed. "I do what I want to do."

"I won't allow it."

"Look. I found the note and the gun. I risked being drowned or shot to bring you that information." She laughed shakily. "I feel like I have a vested interest in keeping you alive."

Once again, his hands came down on her shoulders, his fingers pressing into her skin gently but firmly. "I'm a trained SEAL. I'm used to being shot at. When was the last time someone tried to kill you?"

Her back ramrod straight, she tilted her chin upward. "The last time I drove on I-10 to New Orleans." She touched a hand to his chest. "There are no guarantees in life. For the first time, I've stuck my neck out, and I refuse to bury my head in the sand again."

Sawyer's lips twitched. "Your fiancé was so wrong about you. You know that, don't you?"

Jenna refused to be sidetracked by his sexy grin and the way his eyes shone when he smiled. "You're avoiding the subject."

"You are not a bit boring. Annoyingly protective, but never boring." He bent to touch his forehead to hers. "I'm not taking you with me this time." Sawyer straightened. "But I'll give you my cell phone number in case you run into problems."

She started to open her mouth to argue with him, but he touched a finger to her lips.

"I promise not to go by my bungalow," he continued. "I'll get the case to my guy another way."

Jenna drew in a deep breath and let it out. "I'd rather go with you."

"Sweetheart, I like you, and I like being around you. If we were two people on a regular vacation, I'd rather you came with me, too. But we're not. Please stay here. And remain vigilant in case the gunman figures out what happened to his case."

"Fine," she said. She'd stay long enough for him to leave. Then she'd do whatever she pleased.

Sawyer's eyes narrowed. "My mother always said 'fine' when the situation was anything but fine."

"I'll stay," she said.

He stared at her a moment longer, then nodded. "Where's your cell phone? I want to give you my number and the numbers for my buddies in case something happens to me."

"See? You do need someone with you at all times to keep something from happening to you."

He shook his head and held out his hand. "Your phone?"

She marched to the table where she'd dropped her purse and dug out her cell phone, handing it to him.

He keyed in several numbers and names, then handed it back. "I'll contact you later to let you know I'm alive and I've passed off the case."

"Thanks." She hugged the phone to her chest, her heart heavy at the thought of Sawyer leaving. For the few short hours she'd known him, she'd gotten used to having him around. But she didn't have a real reason to stay with him. She'd done her best to warn him about the threat to his life. It was up to Sawyer to heed the warning and stay alive.

Then why did she feel more alone than ever when he left the bridal suite?

Jenna stared at the closed door, her heart thumping hard against her ribs. Sawyer Houston wasn't her responsibility, but a part of her left with him. Her instincts were screaming at her to go after him. He was in dire danger.

But he was a grown man and a navy SEAL. What could a jilted accountant do to protect him from an assassin?

Chapter Five

As soon as Sawyer left Jenna's suite, he called his wing-man, Dutton Calloway.

"Hey, Sawyer, wanna rent some fishing poles and do some shore fishing this evening?"

"I thought you and Natalie weren't surfacing from your bungalow for the duration of this vacation?"

"That was the general idea. But we were thinking about coming up for air and getting in some fishing."

"Duff, as much as I'd love to do that, I need your help." Sawyer explained what had happened with Jenna and the case containing the rifle and the note. "If someone is truly after me, I need to find out who. I can't walk around in the open without marking myself with a great big bull's-eye."

"Damn, bro." Duff's easygoing attitude of a moment before turned serious. "Where are you now?"

"In the stairwell of Jenna's hotel, two over from ours."

"I'll gather the gang and meet you."

"Where?" Sawyer asked. "I can't stand out in the open."

"Meet ya at the dock. You know which boat."

Sawyer knew the boat Duff mentioned. Natalie's boss had some influence. One of the perks of having him as a boss was the use of a boat belonging to one of his rich friends. They'd used the forty-foot luxury yacht in a res-cue operation to save her.

The boat had gotten them onto the island and…well…it was beautiful and luxurious. What better place to schedule a clandestine meeting?

"Gotcha. See you there in fifteen?" Sawyer paused. "And by gathering the gang, you don't intend to arrive in a group, do you? I don't want the gunman to follow you to me."

"Hey," Duff said. "We're experienced SEALs."

"And we're supposed to be on vacation."

"I know. This is the second unsanctioned operation we've conducted since we've been here."

Sawyer shook his head even though Duff couldn't see him. "Less than a week and we're fighting battles when we should have been sipping mai tais on the beach, served by beautiful waitresses in bright bikinis."

"Yeah. There's something wrong with this picture," Duff agreed. "See ya in fifteen." He ended the call.

Pulling his cap low, Sawyer kept his head tilted down. With the shadows provided by his cap bill and the large mirrored shades, he was nondescript. No one would look twice.

The bottom of the stairwell gave him the option of entering the lobby or exiting the building on the side. He left the building, coming out in a concrete parking lot. The marina was a mile away. He could walk that in fifteen minutes, easy.

Glancing left then right, he hurried away from the resort hotel and out onto the beach. Ideally he would move fast enough that no one could get a bead on him from one of the windows in the high-rise hotels. He needed to get to his own clothing and out of the New Orleans Saints football jersey. If someone recognized him, it would be too easy to follow him in the distinct white jersey with gold-and-black accents.

Thirteen minutes later, he arrived at the marina, having

zigzagged from the beach to the street and finally to the marina. He spotted the Jeep that Montana had rented. He wondered if Quentin would be there with Carly.

He marched on, carrying the big beach bag, trying to look like a tourist preparing to go out on a fancy yacht. When he reached the yacht, he leaped on board and dropped down the stairs into the living quarters.

"About time you got there," Montana announced.

Duff stood beside a smoky-gray quartz table, his arms crossed over his chest. "Quentin took Carly out dancing. He won't be back for a while."

"What gives?" Montana asked.

Sawyer tipped his head toward Montana, and then his gaze slid to Duff.

Duff returned the look, concern drawing his brows together. "We just got here. I haven't filled him in on much."

"Where's Natalie?"

"I left her at the bungalow," Duff said. "She had a conference call with her boss."

"She going back to the Stealth Ops group?" Montana asked.

Duff nodded. "Now that her sister doesn't need her around anymore, she'll report for duty with SOS when she gets back from Cancún next week."

Natalie had told them SOS stood for Stealth Operations Specialists. They were a secret government organization established to take care of anything that needed even more secrecy than the FBI or CIA could provide.

"Thanks for ditching the WaveRunner way down the beach from where we rented it," Montana said. "By the way, who was the babe who jumped on with you?"

"That's why you're here and not at the bungalows." Sawyer pulled the case from the beach bag, laid it on the table and held out his hand. "Got a knife?"

Duff pulled out a slim pocketknife and handed it to Sawyer.

Montana asked, "What's in the case?"

"Trouble," Duff answered for Sawyer.

Sawyer flipped the latches open and lifted the lid, exposing the dark clothing on top.

"I don't get it."

"Give me a sec." Sawyer ran his finger over the spot Jenna had rubbed earlier, and the divider between the top and bottom halves of the suitcase popped upward. When he lifted it all the way, Montana stood.

"What the hell?" He reached for the rifle parts. "You could spend a lot of time in a Mexican jail if they caught you with that kind of equipment." He shot a puzzled glance at Sawyer.

"It's not mine."

"Whose is it? The woman who kidnapped you on the WaveRunner?"

"No. She thought it was her case, took it to her room and discovered the rifle and this." He pulled out the envelope and showed them the photos and the note. "Apparently, someone wants me dead."

Duff grabbed the note, and Montana leaned over his shoulder to read it.

When he finished, Duff shook his head. "But why?"

Sawyer's lips tightened. He suspected the reason had something to do with his father. "If I knew, I might also figure out who could be gunning for me." He paced away from his teammates and back. "All I have are the rifle, the photos and the note." He glanced at Duff. "Has Lance left his bungalow yet?"

Lance had come to Cancún with Natalie to provide SOS technical support in Natalie's mission to find her sister and the other women who'd been abducted. He was a top-notch techno guru with the ability to hack into just about anything.

Duff nodded. "He asked his boss if he could delay his return by two days to catch some of these tropical rays before he returns to his cave in the DC area."

"Do you think he could run a fingerprint check on the rifle?"

"You'll need to provide yours and Jenna's so he can rule them out."

Sawyer frowned. "She didn't handle the rifle, but if he wants to lift prints from the inside of the case and the contents of the envelope... I guess I could go back and get hers."

"You spent part of the day with a woman who hijacked you on a WaveRunner." Duff gave him a hard stare. "Why hesitate now?"

Running a hand through his hair, Sawyer couldn't help but grin. "Actually, she was very nice. Quentin and I met her on the zip-line excursion earlier today."

"Does she have any connection to the woman Quentin took dancing?"

Sawyer nodded. "Roommates and best friends."

Duff tucked the photos and note back into the envelope. "We need to get these to Lance ASAP. The sooner he runs those prints, the better."

"They may come up blank," Montana said. "An experienced assassin wouldn't leave prints on his weapon, would he?"

"You would think he wouldn't leave his case with his gun lying around for a stranger to take, either."

Duff glanced up. "Speaking of which, where *did* Jenna get the case?"

"From the lobby between the concierge and reception desks," Sawyer replied. "Why?"

"It's a pretty modern resort. They probably have a good security system."

Sawyer nodded. "I noticed cameras in the hallways and the stairwells. Stands to reason they'd have them in the lobby."

"I'll ask Lance to hack into their system," Duff said. "He could do that while he's waiting for the match on the latent prints."

"In the meantime, you should be thinking about who you pissed off." Montana grinned. "Maybe it's one of the terrorists we ousted in the Honduras operation."

Sawyer frowned. "If that were the case, why target only me? You'd think whomever was mad about how that went down would go after all of us."

Montana scratched his chin. "That's the case for every one of our missions. It doesn't make sense. Why would anyone pick on only you? What makes you so different?"

Sawyer could think of one thing, but he didn't mention it, because it didn't seem to have any bearing on what was happening in Cancún. Still, he would make a call as soon as he left the boat and his friends.

"For whatever reason they want Sawyer," Duff said, "he can't just walk around in the open. He's tall enough that he would stick out in a crowd. He might as well wear a target on his back. A good assassin with the right tools could easily take him out, even at a distance."

Sawyer's lips twisted. "Thanks, Duff. You're not helping my peace of mind."

"I'm just saying, you can't walk around Cancún without protection." Duff's brows dipped. "At least our assassin has lost his high-powered rifle."

"What you need is a flak jacket. I bet Lance has one in his stash of equipment he brought along with him," Montana offered. He glanced around the boat. "Or we might find one on the boat. It has a better arsenal than we have back on base. Wait here. I'll see if I can find a vest." Montana headed for the back of the boat, where they'd found rifles, handguns and explosives in an arsenal that would make Gunny salivate. Their gunnery sergeant back in Mississippi made it his purpose to obtain the best weapons available on the market for their unit and missions. He'd find everything he could ask for here.

"And I'd hide a flack vest under my loose-fitting Saints jersey?" Sawyer darted a downward glance at the shirt Jenna had loaned him. "I don't think so. We have to find the assassin before he finds me in the crosshairs of whatever weapon he can get his hands on."

Montana shook his head. "The sooner we can get back to Lance with this case, the sooner we can get him started hacking into the resort security system."

"Right." Sawyer glanced around. "I don't suppose Natalie's boss would mind if I camped out here while I'm waiting for an assassin to put a bullet through me."

"I'm sure it would be all right." Duff stared at Sawyer. "How do you want us to go about getting Jenna's fingerprints to compare against those Lance finds on the case and its contents?"

Montana grinned. "I can drop by her room and get them."

Sawyer bristled. "Like hell you will."

"Remember, you can't just waltz in and out of the resorts. You're a wanted man."

"I got out, didn't I?" Sawyer pulled the ball cap over his head and stuck the sunglasses on his nose. "Besides, in Jenna's hotel, I'm her newlywed husband, Mr. Jenna Broyles."

Both Duff and Montana grinned.

"I've heard of love at first sight," Duff drawled, "but marriage at first sight? Isn't that taking it a bit far?"

Sawyer's chest tightened at the thought of being Jenna's

husband for real. He could do worse. She was pretty, spunky and smart. He loved her dark red hair and the way it felt when he sifted his fingers through the silken strands. "Had to come up with a good cover, going up and down the elevator with her. And she's got the bridal suite."

Duff's forehead wrinkled. "Why?"

Sawyer grunted. "Jilted at the altar. She was supposed to be here on her honeymoon, but the bastard didn't know how good he had it."

"Wow. Crappy way to spend your honeymoon," Montana said.

"Yeah. And now, she could be a target if the gunman learns she was the one to find his case."

"You think there's a chance he'll connect her to his missing case?"

"As much of a chance as we have to find him," Duff said, his steady gaze locking with Sawyer's.

"I didn't want to have to go back to Jenna's resort."

"You don't want her to end up collateral damage."

"Exactly." But now that he'd talked himself into going back to the resort and Jenna, he wanted to be there immediately. His belly tightened at the thought of the dangers she might face because of him. "I'm heading back. Let me know what Lance finds."

"Will do." Duff stuck out a hand.

Sawyer took it and shook.

Duff pulled him into a man hug and then let him go. "Later."

"You bet."

With the cap on his head and the shades across on his nose, Sawyer looked like any other tourist who happened to be a New Orleans Saints football fan. He'd have to figure out how to sneak back into his room without being seen to grab a change of clothes. In the meantime, he wanted to get back to Jenna. Now.

Even though they'd found her case before the assassin did, Sawyer didn't have the level of confidence he needed to think Jenna was perfectly safe.

Montana and Duff dropped the case into the beach bag and climbed the steps to exit the boat's hold, leaving Sawyer there alone. Before he went back to Jenna's hotel, he had a call to make.

He touched his smartphone and brought up his emergency contacts, then hit the number at the bottom of the list. The last person he wanted to call when he was in trouble. But this…relationship…was the only striking difference between his teammates and himself that might hold a clue to why he was being targeted.

The line rang three times before someone answered. "Sawyer. Thank goodness, it's you."

The tension in the voice on the other end of the line made Sawyer tighten his hand on the phone. "Senator, have you got anything you want to tell me? Anything I need to know?"

"As a matter of fact, son, I do. Can you make it to DC by morning?"

"No," he said, his tone flat, emotionless. Just like his father's usual demeanor toward him.

"Then I'll come to you," his father said, his voice not nearly as confident and forceful as usual. "There are some things you need to know."

Sawyer ground his teeth together. "Could you start with why I'm being targeted by an assassin?"

AFTER SHE'D CHANGED, Jenna left the bridal suite and descended to the restaurant level. She'd sat alone and picked at a beautifully prepared salad, wasting most of it before she wandered over to the bar, where a reggae band played upbeat music that didn't manage to lift the blue funk settling over Jenna.

In the bar she spotted the man who had been wearing the blue polo shirt earlier that day. Now dressed in a nice pair of black trousers and a white button-up shirt, he sat staring into his glass of beer. When he looked up, his gaze found hers and narrowed.

Although her pulse accelerated, she told herself any good assassin wouldn't so openly glare at her. Still, she questioned her decision to get out and enjoy herself. But now that she was there, she could hardly scurry back to her room. Anyone watching her would know she was nervous. So Jenna found a corner table and sat with her back to the wall. Color her paranoid, but she was damned if someone snuck up on her, especially the guy staring at her full-on.

When he didn't look away, Jenna's ire hitched up. She lifted her chin and glared back at the rude man, giving him every bit of attitude he seemed to be giving her.

Just when she'd had enough staring at the man, he stood and walked across the floor toward her.

Holy hell. Jenna wasn't prepared to die. If he had a gun with a silencer, he could shoot her there in the bar while the band's music drowned out the light thump. She'd seen the movies. Knew just what it sounded like. Heck, he could probably shoot her without pausing and no one would think twice about her slumping over the table—just another drunk tourist.

She ducked her head and pretended she didn't see him approach. From the corner of her eye, she noted every detail of what he was wearing. She searched his hands for a gun and checked for telltale lumps beneath his suit jacket. Was he wearing a shoulder holster with a handgun tucked neatly inside?

Then he was standing right next to her, forcing her to glance upward. "Would you like to dance?"

What she thought he would say and what he did were so divergent, Jenna could only stare and nod, unable to form a coherent thought.

He held out his hand.

As if on autopilot, she placed hers in his and let him draw her to her feet.

"My apologies if I stared at you today," he said as he drew her into his arms and moved to the music. "You remind me of someone."

"Oh, yeah?" Jenna finally found her voice, marveling at how normal she sounded. "Who would that be?"

He didn't answer immediately, swaying to the lilting melody. Then he slowed and stared down into her face, coming slowly to a stop. "My wife."

Jenna stepped backward. "Your wife? Shouldn't you be dancing with her?"

He gave her half a smile. "I would, if she was here. We planned this vacation a year ago." He started to move again, his gaze drifting over Jenna's shoulder as if he didn't see her there at all. "She would have loved it here," he whispered.

Jenna sensed a deep sadness in the man and she asked, "Why didn't she come?"

"She died of breast cancer two months ago."

Her tension bled away in the face of his obvious sorrow, and she scratched him off her list of possible assassins. "I'm so sorry for your loss. My mother died of breast cancer when I was twelve."

"That's tough on a kid. My wife suffered a lot at the end, and it was a relief for her to let go."

"But it wasn't a relief to you," Jenna finished for him.

He gave her a crooked smile and held open his arms. "I

promised you a dance, not a pity party. Let's show these people how to dance to reggae."

In an attempt to cheer the man, Jenna threw herself into mastering the reggae beat. By the time the song ended, she and her dance partner were laughing.

Jenna stuck out her hand. "I'm Jenna Broyles."

"Stan Keeting."

"What was your wife's name?"

"Angela."

"We can dedicate that last dance to Angela."

He smiled. "She would have liked that."

"Thank you for the dance, Stan."

"No." He held her hand a little longer. "Thank you. You made me realize Angela would want me to get on with my life and live it to the fullest."

"I'm glad to hear that." She pulled her hand away and retreated to her table and the watery drink she'd left.

Her gaze snagged on dark-haired Becca, who strode across the barroom floor wearing a silvery dress that hugged every inch of her body and came down to midthigh.

When she spotted Jenna, she crossed to where she sat. "I'm surprised your new husband let you come to the bar alone." She nodded to the empty chair. "Or are you saving this seat for him?"

Jenna's pulse kicked up a notch as she concocted a lie about why she was there without Sawyer. "He was taking a nap. I left a note for him to join me when he woke." She glanced toward the entrance. "I expected to see him by now. I guess he was more exhausted than even he knew." Settling back in her chair, she smiled. "No worries. I'll just finish my drink and join him."

Becca sighed. "You two must be so in love."

Heat rose in Jenna's neck and suffused her cheeks. "It's wonderful." Or at least she thought it would be.

Now that she had some time and distance between her and her ex-fiancé, she realized she'd never really been in love with Tyler. While all of her friends were getting married and having children, she'd fallen in love with the idea of marriage and rushed Tyler into making a commitment neither of them had really been ready for. In effect, he'd done her a favor by jilting her. He'd saved her the heartache and expense of a divorce later.

"I take it he's not the jealous type."

Jenna really didn't know Sawyer well enough to guess. "Why do you ask?"

Becca tipped her head toward Stan, who sat at the bar with a beer in his hand, not drinking, just staring into space. "You two danced well together. I can't say that I've ever danced to reggae."

Jenna smiled. "Stan's a nice man. Maybe he could show you some moves." Her smile slipped. "He lost his wife recently." She glanced down at her drink, suddenly depressed about being alone. She lifted her glass to her lips and sipped. The drink was so watery it no longer had the same appeal as when it was first served.

Jenna had no desire to drink it or to stay in a bar full of strangers. What she really wanted was to see Sawyer again. She pushed away from the table and rose. "It was nice chatting with you, but I think I'll go check on my groom."

Becca nodded and stood, too. "Sleep well."

"You, too." Jenna left the bar, crossed the lobby and punched the button for the elevator. As she waited, she had the distinct feeling someone was watching her. She turned around and stared at the people milling about the lobby. Each one of them was involved in another conversation, with the reception desk, with a companion or on a cell phone. No one was looking her way.

The bell rang, announcing the arrival of the elevator, and the doors slid open.

Jenna stepped in and turned around to press the button for the penthouse floor. When she glanced up, she saw a man in a New Orleans Saints football jersey, a baseball cap and sunglasses enter the lobby and head toward the elevator. Her heart skipped several beats, and a storm of butterflies fluttered inside her belly.

Sawyer.

When he spotted her, he sped up.

About that time, the doors started to slide together.

Jenna scrambled to find the door-open button, and she jammed her finger on it, holding it until Sawyer entered the car. Then she let go and the doors closed.

"I thought you weren't coming around," she said, her voice breathy and unlike her normal confident tone. What was wrong with her? He was just a man. A man with broad shoulders and deep, dark brown eyes she could fall into every time.

He opened his arms. "Even if I didn't have a real reason to come back, I couldn't have stayed away."

Jenna took a step toward him, afraid she'd misread his intention until she was close enough that he gripped her arms and pulled her against him.

"For someone I've only known for today," he said, "I can't seem to get you off my mind."

"Ditto," she mumbled against the New Orleans Saints jersey she'd loaned him. It no longer smelled of her detergent and fabric softener. The shirt held his scent, a hint of rugged, heady, masculine musk and the salty sea air. She inhaled, committing that unique smell to memory.

The elevator car rose to the top floor without another

word being spoken. When the bell rang and the door slid open, Sawyer checked the corridor before letting her step out.

When they arrived at the door to the bridal suite, he held out his hand for her key card, scanned the card and shoved the door open.

Once through, he closed the door behind them and pulled her into his arms, his mouth crashing down on hers, his tongue sweeping in to claim hers.

This was where Jenna had wanted to be all evening. Not eating alone, dancing with a widower or talking to another woman she didn't know or care to know. She'd wanted to be in Sawyer's arms, her heart beating close to his, his mouth melded with hers.

Yes, he was the target of an assassin, and she could be putting herself in the line of fire, but she didn't care as long as Sawyer held her close like this and made love to her all night long. Tomorrow would be soon enough to get to know him better and find whoever was tasked with eliminating her SEAL.

Chapter Six

Sawyer's conversation with his father hadn't yielded enough information to determine who might be after him. The senator insisted he needed to meet with him in person. In the meantime, Sawyer still had an unidentified assassin after him.

All the way back to the resort, Sawyer told himself he would get the fingerprints he needed and leave. Staying with Jenna wasn't an option. Being so near put her at risk. He couldn't let her get hurt because of him.

However, the moment he'd stepped into the lobby of the hotel and saw that flash of auburn hair in the elevator, his heart raced, and he couldn't wait to get her alone. Now that he had her in her suite, he didn't want to leave.

He kissed her, tasting her, feeling her body beneath his fingertips, wanting to get closer, but afraid he'd frighten her by moving too fast.

And there was the matter of being the target of an assassin. He couldn't push that completely out of his mind. After slaking his initial thirst for her, he lifted his head and stared down into her bright green eyes. "You're beautiful, and for some reason, I can't get enough of you."

She chuckled softly, the sound gravelly and sexy as hell. "Funny. I feel the same. And I've never felt that way about anyone before. Especially a virtual stranger."

He cupped the back of her head and pressed a kiss to her forehead, each of her cheekbones and the tip of her nose. "Why is it I don't feel like we're strangers? It's as though I've always known you."

"But you don't know me."

"You're brave and sexy."

"What's my favorite color?" she asked, her eyes closing as he pressed kisses to her eyelids.

"Not important." He brushed her lips with his and skimmed the line of her jaw. "You're gutsy and exciting."

"What do I do for a living?"

"Not important," he repeated. "You have the cutest dimples when you smile, and your eyes twinkle, making them shine so brightly."

She grinned up at him. "Where do I live?"

"In my mind, in my thoughts. In my arms." He tightened his hold, bringing her hips flush up against his. The hard ridge beneath his shorts pressed into her belly. He wanted more. "Your favorite football team is the Saints and you can kiss like nobody's business. What more do I need to know?"

She laughed and rose on her toes to press her lips to his. "You're right. What more do you need to know?" Jenna took his hand and backed toward the bedroom. "Now that you're here, maybe you could stay awhile."

He started to follow her but stopped, his shoulders sagging. "I can't. I came to get your fingerprints. My guy needs to match yours and mine to rule them out before he can run the others on the case through the fingerprint databases."

Jenna nodded, her expression tightening. "Okay. Let's do this." She glanced around the room. "What did you have in mind? I'm fresh out of an ink pad."

"I'll use my cell phone."

Her brows dipped. "Cell phone?"

"Sure. The camera on the phone is sufficient to take a good image of all of your fingers. And it'll take a digital image, which will save my guy time in the transfer." He pulled the waterproof bag out of his back pocket, reminding himself he needed to get fresh clothes soon.

He walked her over to a wall and had her hold each hand up, palm facing the camera, while he took several shots. When he was satisfied the images were sufficiently detailed, he sent the photos to Duff, who would see they made it to Lance.

"That was easier than smudging in ink. And no messy cleanup."

He nodded, staring at her for a long moment, thinking how hard it was going to be leaving her again. "I guess I should go. I only came back to get the prints."

She gave him a small, tight smile. One he hated seeing because again, he sensed her disappointment.

"Where will you go? You can't go back to your bungalow and you can't stay with your friends. That would be the first place the gunman would look."

"I can't stay here," he said.

"Why not?" She tilted her head, her eyes narrowing. "The way I see it, you don't have much of a choice. I have my case, which means the shooter won't know I got his. You're safer here than you are wandering the streets of Cancún in the dark."

He frowned. Maybe he could stay. But did she mean for him to take the couch or join her in the bed? His body tightened, but then he shook his head. "I need fresh clothes."

She shrugged. "I probably have another shirt big enough for you. I brought one to wear over my swimsuit."

"I still need pants."

Jenna smiled. "Can't help you there."

Sawyer shook his head. "I don't want to put you in danger."

"I told you—"

"Yeah, the shooter wouldn't know to look here and it's your choice." He closed the distance between them and cupped the back of her head. "You're making it really hard for me to walk away," he said, his voice roughening.

Jenna slid her hands up his chest and locked them behind his neck. "Then don't."

"I'm not good boyfriend material."

She shook her head and pressed a finger to his lips. "I'm not looking for a boyfriend. I had one. He ran out on me the day of our wedding. Why would I want to do that again?"

He grabbed her hand and removed her finger from his lips. "You're a nice woman. I'd be using you."

Again, she lifted on her toes, this time silencing him with a kiss. "Have you considered I might be using you?"

"Then we'd be even." He kissed her back and pulled her hips against his. "No regrets in the morning?"

"None." A small smile played on her lips. "So, are you staying?"

"For a while."

She shrugged. "Good enough."

"But I want to rinse the sea salt off my skin."

"Help yourself." She waved her hand toward the bathroom and walked away. "We have champagne."

"I'd rather have beer, but champagne will do."

"It'll be waiting when you're through in the shower." She walked toward the living area, pulled the loose cork out of the bottle and poured sparkling liquid into a champagne flute.

Sawyer strode to the bathroom, hoping Jenna would join

him in the shower. She'd invited him to stay in her room, not to make love to her, but if she came into the shower, she'd remove all doubt.

Shucking his swim shorts and the New Orleans Saints shirt, he stepped into a huge shower. What a shame he was the only one inside. Squirting a line of shampoo from the courtesy bottle, he lathered his hair and body, standing in the pulsing spray from the showerhead, getting harder the more he thought about the woman in the room on the other side of the door.

With his life in danger, and hers by default, he had no business thinking of anything but the problem at hand. Instead, his mind went to Jenna's body pressed against his and her lips, velvety soft, yet firm and passionate.

Ducking his head beneath the spray, he reached for the handle to turn the temperature down. Before he could do that, a pair of hands slid around his waist, and soft breasts pressed into his back.

Sawyer groaned.

Jenna's hands stilled. "Was that a good groan or a 'get the heck out of my shower' groan?"

He turned in her arms, the evidence of his desire obvious and prodding her belly. "I was just thinking about you."

Her eyes widened and she lifted her face to accept his kiss.

Sawyer threaded his hands in her hair and tugged, tipping her head so that he could trail kisses down the side of her neck and lower to the swells of her breasts. He scooped her up by the backs of her thighs, wrapping her legs around his waist.

Jenna rested her hands on his shoulders. "You have protection?"

He moaned. "Yes." Setting her back on her feet, he dived out of the shower and grabbed for the waterproof container, yanking it open so fast, his cell phone and wallet flew across the counter.

A giggle behind him only made his fingers move faster. Finally he found what he was looking for in a dark foil packet. Back inside the shower, he ripped open the packet and removed its contents.

She took it from him and slowly rolled it down over his shaft, her fingers circling him, her touch gentle, as she made her way down his length to the base.

Past control, he lifted her, pressing her back against the cool tile wall.

She wrapped her legs around his waist again and lowered herself over him as he thrust upward, gliding into her warm, wet channel, filling her all the way.

Jenna drew in a long, deep breath and held it as he froze, giving her body time to adjust to his length and girth. When she pressed down on his shoulders and eased up, he pulled out to the very tip and thrust back inside.

With Jenna leveraging herself on his shoulders and Sawyer pumping in and out, they settled into a smooth, fast rhythm, the pace increasing until a firestorm of electricity ripped through Sawyer.

Jenna tensed and called out his name. "Sawyer!"

One final thrust and Sawyer spent himself inside her, buried deep, wrapped in her tightness.

When at last he could think again, he lowered her to her feet, grabbed the bar of soap and lathered her entire body, memorizing every curve and dimple, every edge and angle until he had her covered in suds. Then he swung her beneath the spray and rinsed her off.

"My turn." Jenna returned the favor, her fingers skimming over the muscles of his back and shoulders, down his chest and around to the curve of his bottom. When she came back around to his front, he was amazed at how quickly he'd recovered from their first round. "Let's take it into the bedroom."

"Better yet, let's take it into the hot tub." She helped rinse him off, running her hands all over his body, bumping him with a breast, tempting him with the brush of her hips. Finally she reached around him and shut off the water. "Ready?"

"More than you can imagine."

She glanced down and winked. "It doesn't take much of an imagination to see that." Then she was out of the shower and streaking naked across the suite to the hot tub in a secluded alcove on the deck outside.

When he slipped into the water beside her, he commented, "Your ex-fiancé was a complete idiot. But remind me to thank him."

"Thank him?" She moved to straddle his lap. "Why?"

"For leaving you at the altar so that I'd find you alone in Cancún. His loss was my gain." He captured her face in his hands and kissed her long and hard while he slid inside her, taking her for the second time that night.

After soaking in the hot tub for twenty minutes, they dried each other off and fell into the king-size bed, exhausted and satiated.

Jenna fell asleep curled beside him, her cheek resting on his shoulder, her hand lying on his chest.

Hell, he could get used to this. Way too easily. He lay for a long time holding her naked form against his body, for the first time in his life wishing he could be with a woman for more than a night. For a lot more than just a night.

After the upbringing he'd had with absentee parents who rarely spent time in each other's company, Sawyer had never considered himself good boyfriend or husband material. He hadn't had the best examples set for him. How was he supposed to be the man a woman needed?

And Jenna had said she wasn't in the market for a replacement fiancé. Burned once, she was less likely to fall into that trap again.

Still, Sawyer didn't want to let go of her.

He had drifted into a light sleep when his cell phone buzzed on the nightstand beside him. Careful not to wake Jenna, he checked the text message.

Come to the Bungalow. You need to see this video.

The message was from Duff, who was probably standing over Lance's shoulder in the bungalow near Sawyer's. And then came a second text.

Will position Montana for cover.

Sawyer replied, Roger.

Easing out of the bed, he dressed in his shorts and the New Orleans Saints jersey. He bent to press a kiss to Jenna's lips, his body tightening at that touch.

He hated leaving her. If they found something on the security video that could point them in the direction of his would-be assassin, he had to go. The sooner he put an end to the attempt to abduct or kill him, the sooner he could get on with his life.

Pulling the ball cap down low on his forehead, he pocketed the sunglasses but chose not to wear them unless he had to. In the dark, they would limit visibility. He took the back way out of the resort and jogged along the beach to his hotel complex, keeping a watch on all sides. He didn't want someone surprising him by running up behind him. Once he neared the path leading between a stand of palm trees and the bungalows he and his teammates had rented for their vacation, he slowed.

Something in the shadows moved.

Sawyer dived for the sandy soil, rolled and leaped to his feet, ready to rumble.

A low chuckle made him tense.

"You're getting slow, Sawyer." Montana stepped away from the trunk of a palm. "I did a recon of the path. All clear. You can proceed."

Sawyer brushed the sand off his body, shaking his head. "I'm supposed to be on vacation, not an operation."

"You do what you have to do to stay alive, on vacation or not. We kind of like you on the team." Montana clapped a hand on his shoulder and nodded toward the bungalow. "Go. Lance has something he wants you to see."

Sawyer didn't argue. Trusting his teammate to have his six, he went straight to Lance's bungalow and knocked. Within seconds, Duff yanked open the door. "About time. I thought you were coming straight back after you got Jenna's fingerprints."

"I was distracted."

Duff snorted. "Women can be pretty distracting. I tell you, I'd rather be with Natalie than a bunch of guys staring at a video monitor. Let's get this done so we can actually have a shot at a real vacation."

"You're not going to get any arguments out of me." Sawyer stepped behind Lance. "Thanks for taking on this assignment."

Lance shot a look over his shoulder at Sawyer and returned his attention to the screen. "Not only did the boss give me permission, he also assigned me to you until you don't need my services." The man shrugged. "I can't complain too much. I'm in Cancún. Every once in a while, I step outside and actually see the sun and the beach. I might even get a chance to put my feet in the water when we solve this case."

Sawyer patted Lance's shoulder. "We'll try to make it as short and painless an assignment as we can."

"I'm counting on it." He pointed to the screen. "It took some finagling, but I was able to hack into the resort's security system. Based on what you told us about when she took the wrong case, I was able to get several shots of the lobby right around the time Jenna took the case. Now watch."

He pointed to the screen. "This is the lobby. There's Jenna, and she's heading for the concierge."

Sawyer's chest tightened. Seeing her on the screen made him wish he'd brought her with him rather than leave her lying naked in the bed in her suite. Alone. Potentially vulnerable.

"There's the case standing beside the concierge's stand." Lance tapped the screen.

Sawyer could make out the shape and size of the case. But no one stood close enough to indicate who the case belonged to. "Why is this a big deal? You're not showing me anything different than what Jenna told me."

"We started at this point and then backed up." Lance set the video in rewind, backing up slowly enough that they could make out all the people coming and going in the lobby in reverse motion. For several seconds, the case remained static, apparently left long before Jenna had arrived to claim it mistakenly.

Then a figure moved in front of the concierge, and the case disappeared.

"Wait." Sawyer leaned closer. "Run it forward."

"Hold on. We're working on the resort server, and it can be slow." Lance played the video in forward slow motion. A man walked into the lobby, carrying a case. *The* case. He set it down by the concierge, straightened, glanced around and left through a side door.

"Can you get a clear image of his face?" Sawyer asked.

Lance nodded. "Already did. We're running facial-recognition software on him." Lance switched to a different screen, where an image of the man who'd dropped the case was being compared to a database of potential suspects, flipping through one after another so fast Sawyer could barely keep up.

"What about after Jenna picked up the case? Did anyone else go by the concierge's desk looking for a case?"

"There were several people in the minutes following Jenna's arrival and departure on the scene," Lance said. He switched back to the video from the resort, fast-forwarded to Jenna taking the case and then set the footage in slow motion.

A man wearing jeans and a T-shirt strode across the lobby and stopped at the concierge desk. No one manned the desk. The man looked behind the desk, walked around it, shook his head and left.

A woman in a broad-brimmed hat approached the counter. She set her purse on the counter and dug into it for a moment. The concierge never appeared. The woman found what looked like a powder compact, opened it, applied fresh lipstick, returned her compact and lipstick to her purse and then moved on.

"Can you get a clear shot of the woman's face?" Sawyer asked.

Lance shook his head. "No. All I could get was her chin."

A man dragged a large suitcase up to the concierge's desk and tapped his fingers on the wood. When the concierge finally appeared, he took the case, handed the man a ticket and stowed the case in the room behind him.

"I skimmed through the next hour of footage but didn't find anything else unusual," Lance said.

The image of the hotel lobby blinked out, and an error message displayed on the screen.

"Did you just click off?" Sawyer asked, even though he hadn't seen Lance touch the mouse or keyboard when the screen disappeared.

Lance frowned. "No." He tried to bring up the resort's security system again. "I can't seem to get into the system. Let me try another route." Lance's fingers flew across the keyboard. "There. I've hacked into the registration system. Damn." He clicked a few more keys.

"What?" Sawyer leaned closer to the monitor.

Lance's frown deepened. "I'm getting a message that the fire alarm has gone off. The resort employees are to evacuate the main hotel building."

Sawyer straightened, his chest tightening. "Do you suppose whoever is looking for that case could have hacked into the security system and seen the same footage we did?"

Lance nodded. "It's possible. The system was a breeze to get into for even the clumsiest hacker."

Sawyer sprinted for the door.

"Where are you going?" Duff asked.

"If we saw Jenna pick up that case, the assassin could have seen her, as well. I've got to get to her."

"What if the assassin is using this as a way to lure you out?"

"I can't leave Jenna without protection."

Chapter Seven

Jenna was in the middle of a very sensuous dream with Sawyer when an alarm went off, yanking her out of his dream arms and into reality. She sat up and stared bleary-eyed at the empty pillow beside her. The alarm clock blinked a green 3:46 a.m. Jenna patted the alarm to shut it off, but it kept blaring. "Sawyer?" she called out.

When she was met with nothing but the piercing squall of the continuous alarm, she realized it was the fire alarm in the hallway. She leaped out of the bed and ran to the bathroom, just in case Sawyer was there and hadn't heard her call or the fire alarm's scream.

Sawyer wasn't there, and his clothes were gone.

The persistence of the alarm forced Jenna to take action. She pulled a sundress over her naked body, stepped into panties, slipped on a pair of sandals, grabbed her purse and headed for the door—all in a matter of seconds.

"Fire alarm! All guests must evacuate," a voice announced in the hallway.

Jenna yanked open the door.

Before she could take a step out, someone dressed completely in black came at her, hunched over like a linebacker. He plowed into her belly and lifted her off her feet, carrying her back into the room.

She screamed, but the door to her room closed, her cry for help drowned out by the fire alarm.

The man threw her on the bed.

Her heart racing, Jenna rolled over to the other side, dropping her feet to the floor.

The man in black ran around the end of the bed and grabbed for her.

Jenna somersaulted back across the mattress and hooked her hands in the comforter.

When the man launched himself across the bed, she dragged the comforter over his head and twisted it, wrapping him in the fabric. Then she ran for the door and yanked it open.

Footsteps pounded after her.

Unable to slam the door behind her, she ran as fast as she could, pushing through the exit door leading into the stairwell. Running downward, she took two steps at a time, braced her hands on the railing and vaulted at the turn, landing four steps lower.

From the tenth floor, she ran down the ninth, then the eighth. Other guests flowed into the stairwell. She pushed past them and kept running. When she reached the sixth floor, she ran into Becca, who was working her way up the stairs. She stopped in front of Jenna, forcing her to come to a halt.

Jenna shot a glance up the stairs, her heart pounding and her breathing coming in ragged gasps.

Becca gripped her arm. "Jenna? What's wrong?"

"Someone attacked me."

"Where?" Becca looked over Jenna's shoulder. Guests dressed in bathrobes and pajamas marched down the stairs, wide-eyed and worried.

"In my room."

"Let's get you out of here." Becca cast another glance

up the stairs and then turned. She put an arm around Jenna and hurried her down to the ground floor and out the back of the resort near the pool.

People milled around the grounds, clutching each other and staring at the hotel, searching for the smoke expected with a fire.

"I need to report the assault," Jenna said, looking around for the hotel security staff, a Cancún police officer or anyone she could tell about the attack. Still shaking, she wondered if the man was actually walking among them, merging with the frightened guests leaving the building.

When they finally came to a stop near the outdoor bar, Becca gripped Jenna's arms. "Are you all right?"

Jenna rubbed her hands over her arms and shivered. "I think I am."

"What happened?"

"I don't know." She could barely believe she'd gotten away. "I opened the door and someone rammed into me, then threw me on the bed."

"What did he look like?"

Jenna flung out her hands. "I don't know. He was wearing all black and a black ski mask."

"Did he say what he wanted?"

"No, he just tried to grab me and I…I…got away." Her body trembled in the aftermath of her near miss. If she hadn't been able to slip away, what would have happened?

Her breath caught in her throat, and her heart skittered to a stop. The assassin. He had to be looking for his missing weapon.

"Jenna?" Becca's eyes narrowed. "Are you sure he didn't say anything?"

"He didn't say anything." Jenna had to get to Sawyer and warn him that the assassin had found her in his attempt to locate his missing weapon. He'd known who she was and where to find her. "I have to go."

"Where?" Becca asked.

"Jenna!" A deep male voice called out from the far side of the crowd gathered around the pool.

Jenna stood on her toes, trying to see over the throng. A tall man, towering over many of the others, emerged from the darkness. "Jenna!"

"Sawyer?" she cried out and ran toward him.

He held open his arms and engulfed her in his embrace. "Whoa, sweetheart, what happened?" He held her close, brushing the hair from her face.

She pressed her mouth to his ear. "We have to leave here. Now."

"Let's go." He curled her into his arm, shielding her body with his, and moved toward the beach.

"Jenna?" Becca called out.

Jenna stopped, feeling guilty for abandoning her new friend without explanation. "I have to go. Thank you for getting me out of there."

"Where are you going? I'm sure someone probably pulled the fire alarm as a prank, but we can report your attacker to the police when they get here."

"I can't stay. I have to go."

Becca nodded. "I understand. Do be careful." She stared past Jenna to Sawyer. "She's had quite a shock."

"I'll take care of her," he promised.

His words warmed her insides, which still trembled from her encounter.

When they escaped the crowd milling around the pool, Sawyer asked, "What happened?"

She told him about the man in the black clothes and mask. "It had to be the guy after the case. But how did he find me?"

Sawyer didn't answer. Instead, he took her hand. "Can you jog?"

"Yes. I work out at home."

"Then come on. We need to get out of the open." He set off at a fairly easy pace, running along the shore near the waves washing up on the harder-packed sand.

They passed one resort, and as they approached the next, two men stepped out of the shadows of a palm tree.

Jenna dug her feet into the sand and backed away, pulling at Sawyer's hand.

He stopped.

"Sawyer," one man said. "It's me, Montana."

"And Duff," the other man said. "Glad you found her before the gunman did."

Jenna shot a glance up at Sawyer, his face visible in the starlight. "You knew he'd come?"

He nodded. "Just a few minutes ago. It's why I came back. We were able to review the security-camera footage from the lobby and saw when you retrieved the case."

"And who came looking for it?"

"That wasn't as clear." Sawyer led her onto a path connecting pretty little bungalows. "The point is, if we could hack into the security system and see the footage…so could the gunman looking for his case."

Jenna's heart dropped into her belly like a heavy weight, and she swayed. If not for Sawyer's arm around her waist, she might have fallen to her knees.

As the moved down the path, another figure appeared out of the shadows, this one with a more feminine shape.

Duff stepped up to the woman and bent to kiss her lips. "I take it the path is clear?"

"For now." She glanced across at Jenna. "This must be Jenna."

Sawyer nodded, leading Jenna through the other three. "Let's get inside, and then we can do the introductions."

They stopped in front of one of the bungalows, and Sawyer knocked. Montana, the woman and Duff stood close behind them, shielding Sawyer's and Jenna's bodies from any potential threat.

The door opened, and a man waved them in. Once they were all inside, he closed the door and turned to take his seat at a desk.

"Jenna, this is Lance," Sawyer said, pointing to the man who'd opened the door.

"Hey." Lance didn't glance up from the two monitors.

"Are you a SEAL, as well?" Jenna asked.

The man snorted. "Not hardly. I work much harder than they do."

Sawyer nodded to his teammate's girlfriend. "Natalie and Lance are special agents."

"What kind of special agents?" Jenna asked. "FBI, CIA, Interpol?"

Natalie chuckled. "None of the above. We work with a top secret agency. That's all I can tell you."

"Or she has to kill you," Lance quipped.

Jenna stared from Lance back to Natalie.

Natalie glared at Lance. "Don't listen to him. He's just grouchy because he's been here four days and has yet to set foot in the water."

"Yeah. While you guys are having all the fun, I'm stuck in my geek cave, doing all the real work." He touched his mouse, and one of the screens lit up. It displayed a somewhat blurry image of a Hispanic man. From what Jenna could tell, he was standing in the lobby of a hotel.

She peered closer. *Her* hotel.

Lance pointed at the screen on the left. "This is the man who left the case with the concierge."

"Is he the gunman?" Jenna asked.

"We don't think so," Sawyer replied.

Lance chimed in, "We think he left the case for the gunman, who would have picked it up if you hadn't snagged it first." He shot a smile at her. "By the way, great job warning Sawyer."

"Yeah," Montana added. "I got to thinking, went back to the rental company and found something that looked suspiciously like a bullet hole in the rear of the WaveRunner you two sped off on."

Sawyer raised his eyebrows at Montana. "When did you do that?"

"While you were out earlier." Montana's glance shifted to Jenna and back. "I haven't had a chance to tell you."

Her throat constricting, Jenna swallowed hard. "Are you sure it was a bullet hole?"

Montana's lips twisted. "I'm sure. When it got nailed into the back of that WaveRunner? I don't know the answer to that. I wasn't looking for bullet holes when we rented it."

Sawyer's fists clenched, his face hardening. He reached for Jenna's hand and pulled her close. "Damn it, Jenna. You should have turned that case over to the police instead of coming after me."

She leaned into Sawyer's hard body, his strength helping her deal with the fact that she could have taken the bullet if the shooter aimed a little higher or they hadn't gotten out to sea fast enough. "It doesn't matter now."

"It sure as hell does. You were attacked tonight. Whoever is after me has now come after you."

"He might have come looking for you and found me instead."

Sawyer gripped her arms. "He attacked you."

"If you two could pay attention for a moment..." Lance

clicked the mouse and the other screen blinked to life, displaying several images of what appeared to be the same man from the hotel in various other places. "I found these on the CIA's database. This man is one the CIA and DEA have been watching. Jorge Ramirez."

"Why?" Sawyer moved closer, staring hard at the man on the screen, memorizing his features. If Ramirez had anything to do with the attack on Jenna, Sawyer would find him and take him out of everyone's misery.

"He works for Carmelo Devita, the same drug runner who had a hand in the human trafficking case we just busted wide-open."

"But Devita wasn't the orchestrator of that operation," Duff said. "He was only hired help to get the job done."

"Question is, who hired Devita this time, and how do we find him? If we can get to Devita, we can figure out who's gunning for me," Sawyer said.

Natalie tapped her chin and narrowed her eyes. "Our boss has other connections here in the Cancún area."

Sawyer's lips curled up at the corners. "I'm not surprised." He raised his hand to Natalie. "Don't worry. I'm not looking that gift horse in the mouth."

Natalie grinned. "Good, because I don't even know half his contacts. He has them all over the world."

Jenna stared at Natalie. "Is your boss on our side? Or is he also involved in criminal activities?"

Her grin disappeared. "Royce is one of the best human beings you'll ever meet. Whatever he does, he does for the good of the people of our country."

Jenna raised her hands. "Okay. I get it."

Natalie stared at Jenna a moment longer and then relaxed. "Sorry. We just got through a pretty hairy situation with a human trafficking operation. I'm a little punchy."

"Are you two through talking?" Lance asked. "The boss sent us an address where we might be able to find Ramirez."

Sawyer's eyes narrowed, and his hand tightened around Jenna's waist. "Good. I'm going."

"Me, too," Duff added.

"Count me in," Montana said. "And Quentin will want to get involved as well when he wraps up his date." The big SEAL shook his head. "Some guys have all the luck."

"I'm just glad my roommate was out with him when the guy attacked me," Jenna said.

"Speaking of which." Sawyer pulled out his smartphone and keyed some letters. "Just texting Quentin to keep your roommate occupied for the night and not let her go back to the room."

"Good. I wouldn't want her to run into the attacker. She hasn't been clued in on the case, the rifle, the attempt on Sawyer's life or my involvement in any of this." Jenna ran a hand through her hair. "Perhaps I should call her and fill her in on all of this. Quentin can probably take good care of her."

Sawyer glanced down at Jenna. "In the meantime, you can't go back to the suite."

"What a waste. I have the best suite in the entire hotel and I can't even use it." Jenna clapped her hands and rocked back on her heels. "So, what's next? Who are we going after, and what do we hope to gain from them?"

"We need to find Devita," Sawyer said. "And the way to find Devita is to follow Ramirez back to him."

"Are we going to wait for Quentin?" Duff asked.

Sawyer shook his head. "I think the three of us can handle this."

"Four," Jenna interjected.

"Quentin isn't coming with us," Sawyer said.

Jenna squared her shoulders and braced her feet slightly apart, preparing for battle. Then faced Sawyer. "*He's* not, but *I* am." Her heart fluttered. The mild-mannered, boring accountant had stood her ground.

"You're not trained for covert operations."

"Maybe not, but that's not the point." She propped a hand on her hip. "Where will I stay while you gentlemen are off interrogating thugs?"

"You can stay here," Lance offered.

"The gunman thinks I have the case with his rifle. And if he put the bullet in that WaveRunner, by now he knows I might be with Sawyer. He'll be looking for me, and what better place to look than near where Sawyer has a room?" She lifted her chin, daring them to argue.

Sawyer frowned. "You're not going. I'll get you another room."

"Where I'll be by myself, unprotected by you big, strong navy SEALs?" She stared up at him in challenge.

Montana coughed. "She has a point."

Sawyer's jaw hardened. "No, she doesn't. Members of the drug cartels are dangerous. They'd just as soon shoot you as look at you." He glared at Jenna. "You're not going."

She nodded. "Very well. I'll just do one of two things. I'll either go back to my hotel and sit in my room, where I might or might not be attacked again, or perhaps I'll hire a taxi, snoop around and ask my own questions about the cartel. That might get me killed, but I've already become a target anyway."

Duff's lips twitched. "She has a point."

"Damn it!" Sawyer grabbed the ball cap Jenna had loaned him and the mirrored sunglasses. "We're wasting time. Let's go."

"You'll stay in the Jeep and keep out of sight while we go in to question Ramirez," Sawyer said, giving her his sternest frown. He still wasn't happy she'd ended up in the backseat of the vehicle with him.

"I want to be there when you question Ramirez."

"No."

"But—"

"We need someone to stay here and guard the car," Duff said. He pulled a nine-millimeter pistol from beneath the front seat. "Know how to use one of these?"

She swallowed, the muscles in her throat convulsing. "Uh. No. Not really."

Sawyer rolled his eyes and then grabbed the weapon from Duff. He pointed to the end of the barrel. "This is the business end of the pistol. Don't point it at anything you don't intend to shoot."

Her brows lowered. "I'm not a complete idiot," she muttered.

"Yeah. Well, I don't plan on being shot accidentally." He glared at Duff and released the magazine from the handle. "And you don't give a loaded weapon to someone who has never fired one before."

Duff grinned. "She's smart. I'm sure she could figure it out."

Sawyer slid the bolt back, cleared the weapon and handed it to Jenna. "If bad guys try to break into the Jeep while you're in here, aim this gun at them."

"Aren't you going to put the bullets back in it?"

"No." He stowed the magazine beneath the seat in front of him. "Just waving the gun will scare them enough to leave you alone."

"Nice of you to decide the best way to protect myself is with an empty weapon," she said, her frown deepening.

"And if I pull the pistol and the other guy has a bigger, badder one with actual bullets…then what?"

"We'll be back before then," he assured her, even though he didn't know how long it would take to find Ramirez and extract the information they needed. All they had was an address. If he was at that location, he might slip out the back before they could get close. If they had to chase him, that would put them even farther away from the Jeep and Jenna.

Sawyer touched Montana's shoulder. "Give her the keys."

"What?" Montana clutched the keys in his fist. "Why?"

"If she needs to get away in a hurry, she'd be better off driving out of the barrio and back to the resorts than going on foot." Sawyer shook his head. "Give her the damn keys."

Jenna's eyes narrowed. "I'm not leaving without you."

Sawyer gripped her shoulders. "You have to do whatever it takes to survive." He gave her a gentle shake. "Do you understand?"

"Yes." She took the keys from Montana. When the men climbed out of the vehicle, she rolled down the window. "Be careful," she whispered.

"Stay out of sight." Sawyer leaned into the Jeep, gripped the back of her head in his palm and kissed her hard on the lips. "Please." Then he left before he decided to stay with her when he had a man to find and question.

Montana had chosen what appeared to be a deserted back alley located two blocks from Ramirez's last known address. Since it was early in the morning, few people were out on the street.

Sawyer took point, followed by Duff and then Montana. They slipped between buildings and cut through alleys, making their way to the address.

"Ramirez's place should be on the next street." Sawyer slowed, eased up to the edge of the alley and peered around the corner of the building. The early-morning sun cast a deep, dark shadow over the alley where he stood, giving him good concealment until he stuck his head out.

People were beginning to stir, waking to a bright, sunshiny morning. With the image of Ramirez firmly in mind, Sawyer pulled his cap low and left the relative safety of the alley. He walked past the wall surrounding the house Royce had indicated was Ramirez's last known residence and ducked around the side.

When he was sure no one was looking, he braced his hands on the top of the adobe wall and pulled himself over, dropping to the hard-packed dirt on the other side. Fortunately, he'd landed on a side of the house with few windows. Crouching low, he eased along the base of the stucco home until he arrived at a window. The scent of grilled beef and tortillas drifted through the open window, making Sawyer's belly grumble, reminding him he hadn't eaten anything since the day before.

He swallowed hard, focusing on what he needed to accomplish. Rising up, he peered over the edge of the windowsill into the kitchen.

A petite Hispanic woman stood at the stove, flipping a tortilla. She called out over her shoulder in Spanish that the food was ready.

A man's voice came from deeper inside the house. From what Sawyer understood, he was telling her to wrap it. He'd take it with him.

The woman filled a tortilla with a scrambled egg and sausage mix, and then folded foil around it. She made two more just like the first and carried them into another room, out of Sawyer's sight.

Sawyer whispered into one of the headsets Lance had outfitted the team with. "I haven't laid eyes on the man of the house, but if it's Ramirez, he's coming out. Be ready."

"Roger," Duff responded. "Spotted an empty building two doors down. We can take him there."

Already on the move, Sawyer crept toward the front of the house, peering into the windows as he went, following the woman's footsteps until they halted and she said something in Spanish that Sawyer couldn't quite catch.

He edged up to the window closest to the front and peered over the ledge into the modest home. The woman handed a woven bag to a man with his back to the window.

Without kissing her or saying another word, he stuffed a pistol under his guayabera, grabbed the handles of the bag and turned toward the door.

Bingo.

The profile of the man matched the one Sawyer had seen in the resort's lobby video. They had their man.

Or rather...they'd located their quarry. They still had to extract him.

Sawyer dropped to his haunches. "It's him."

"Moving in," Montana said.

Ducking beneath the window, Sawyer eased toward the door.

Ramirez exited the house, crossed the small yard and opened the wooden gate.

As soon as the gate swung open, Sawyer rushed forward, silent on his feet, and slipped the gun from beneath Ramirez's shirt.

"Huh?" Ramirez glanced downward.

Sawyer took advantage of Ramirez's surprise by grabbing one of the man's arms and yanking it up the middle of his back. Then he shoved Ramirez out into the street and kicked the gate shut behind him.

The SEALs closed in.

Montana slapped a strip of duct tape over Ramirez's mouth.

With Sawyer still twisting the man's arm up the middle of his back and Duff holding him steady, they maneuvered him into the alley, shuffled to the back of the houses and guided him to the abandoned building. Duff used his knife to break through a lock and pushed the door open.

Once inside, Montana secured Ramirez's wrists by taping them together behind him.

Duff called out, "In here."

Sawyer and Montana shoved Ramirez ahead of them into an office with a table and two rickety wooden chairs.

Sawyer pushed Ramirez into one of the chairs, grabbed the duct tape over Ramirez's mouth and yanked it off with a layer of the man's skin.

Ramirez cried out and cursed in Spanish.

"Where is he?" Sawyer asked.

Their captive squeezed his eyes shut and ran his tongue across his raw lips. When he opened his eyes, his gaze shot daggers at Sawyer. "I should kill you myself," he said in English with a thick accent.

"Where's Devita?"

Ramirez sneered. "No one knows but Devita. You waste your time."

"Then we should just kill you." Sawyer pulled the gun he'd confiscated from Ramirez, cocked it and held it to Ramirez's head.

Montana touched Sawyer's arm. "Let me." He pulled his knife from the scabbard strapped to his calf, the tip razor-sharp. "I've always wanted to do this." He shoved the table in front of Ramirez and sat across from him. "Let me have one of his hands."

Using his knife, Duff sliced through the tape holding Ramirez's wrists together and brought his hands forward. Then he taped one of his wrists to the chair and the other to the tabletop, the fingers splayed out.

Sawyer almost laughed at the maniacal look in Montana's eyes. What Ramirez didn't know was that Montana was an expert with the knife. He'd perfected his skill on hunting trips with his friends in the Crazy Mountains of Montana. When the hunting day was done, they sat around the cabin entertaining each other with knife tricks.

Ramirez stared at the knife in Montana's hand. "What are you going to do?"

"I suggest you remain very still." Montana's hand shot out, and he planted the tip of the knife in the desk between Ramirez's thumb and forefinger.

Ramirez stiffened, his eyes widening.

"Better start talking." In lightning-fast movements, Montana stabbed the knife between Ramirez's fingers, over and over, alternating the pattern, never hitting the man's fingers.

Sawyer leaned close to Ramirez's ear. "When he gets tired, he starts to miss."

Ramirez's eyes grew wider, and sweat beaded on his forehead. "I don't know where Devita is. He sends his people to me."

Montana stabbed the knife so close to one of Ramirez's fingers, he nicked it, drawing blood.

Ramirez cried out. "I do not know!"

Montana went faster.

"Por favor!" Ramirez closed his eyes and sobbed. *"Por favor.* I do not know."

Sawyer touched Montana's shoulder, and the mountain

man slammed the knife into the table one last time, drawing another drop of blood from Ramirez. Then he stood, pulled the knife out of the table and wiped the blood on his pant leg.

Sawyer sat in the chair across from Ramirez. "Tell Devita I'm coming for answers, and he'd better have them. I won't be nearly as neat as my friend with his knife."

"I will tell him, but he will laugh." Ramirez's lip curled. "He has many people. You will not get close to him."

Sawyer stood, his eyes narrowed. Ramirez didn't know anything. He was useless to them. But he might lead them to Devita through his contacts. "Let him go."

Duff yanked the duct tape off the man's wrists, grabbed him by the back of his collar, jerked him to his feet and shoved him out the door, aiming him away from the road where they'd parked the Jeep. "Run."

Ramirez took off running and didn't slow down.

Sawyer turned in the opposite direction. "Let's get back to the Jeep." They'd been gone long enough. He wanted to see Jenna. His instincts were never wrong. They'd saved him in too many operations to count. And right then, they were screaming at him to save Jenna. She was in trouble.

As he sprinted back the way they'd come, he heard the sound of gunfire.

Chapter Eight

Jenna lay on the backseat, peeking out the window every few minutes, counting the seconds until the men returned. Though they'd parked the Jeep in the shade and it was early morning, the outside temperatures were heating up, and so was the interior of the Jeep.

Ten minutes passed and the guys hadn't returned. She stared at her watch as the minutes ticked away like molasses dripping in the wintertime. At the fifteen-minute mark, she bit her lip and dared to look out the window again.

When she popped up, dark eyes stared down at her, and a male voice yelled something in Spanish.

Damn. She's been spotted.

Before she could gather her wits and brandish the gun, three more men appeared, surrounding the Jeep, talking in rapid-fire Spanish. One of them raised a tire iron.

Jenna jerked her hand up and aimed the pistol at the man with the tire iron. "Stop or I'll shoot," she yelled.

The men laughed and pointed at the gun in her hand. They must have somehow known it was empty.

Jenna's heart sank and her pulse spiked as the man with the tire iron raised it high and slammed it into the passenger window, spewing glass all over the inside of the vehicle.

Jenna dived for the floorboard, where Sawyer had dropped the magazine full of bullets. Where was it?

The man poked the tire iron through the window and used it to clean out the jagged edges of the glass.

Covered in pieces of window glass, Jenna searched feverishly for the magazine, her fingers finally closing around the cool metal. She jammed it into the handle of the pistol and rolled to her back as one of the men reached inside and opened the door.

Jenna pointed at the man's leg and pulled the trigger.

The gun went off, jerking back in her hand.

The man in the door screamed, grabbed his leg and toppled backward, crashing to the ground. The other three men backed away, holding their hands in the air.

Jenna eased up on the seat and waved the gun at the man on the ground. "Take him and go," she said, her voice shaking almost as much as her hands.

Two of the men rushed forward, grabbed their friend under the arms and dragged him away.

Jenna didn't lower the gun until the men disappeared around the corner. Then she scrambled across the center console into the driver's seat, fumbled getting the key into the ignition, dropped it and had to fish it off the floor. When she finally had the key in the ignition, she twisted it. The Jeep lurched and died.

What the hell? She stared down at the shift on the floor and almost cried. She'd forgotten the vehicle was a standard shift, and she hadn't driven one since she was a freshman in high school and even then only in a flat, empty parking lot.

She glanced around for the men who'd broken the window. When she ascertained the coast was clear, she laid the gun on the seat and gripped the shift, scraping through her memory for how to drive without an automatic transmission.

Jenna placed both feet onto the pedals on the floor, remembering one was the brake, the other the clutch. With the clutch pressed to the floor, she twisted the key in the ignition, and the vehicle hummed to life.

"Oh, thank God." She shifted the gear into First and eased her foot off the clutch and onto the gas. The Jeep jumped forward, rolling up on the curb and back down, jolting her insides.

If anyone reported the gunshot, it wouldn't be long before the Mexican police arrived. She had to leave with or without Sawyer, Montana and Duff. They were fully capable of finding a ride back to the resort, and Jenna didn't want them to be blamed for her shooting someone. If anyone was going to jail, it would be her.

Still, she didn't want to leave without knowing what had happened. The men could be in serious trouble. They could have run into more of Devita's men than they were prepared to fight off. Perhaps she could drive past Ramirez's house in case they needed a getaway car.

The engine built to a crescendo and Jenna slammed her foot to the clutch, shifted into second gear and popped the clutch loose. The Jeep jerked and trembled, threatened to die, then chugged into second. As she neared the intersection taking her out of the alley, three men skidded around the corner.

Jenna nearly cried with relief.

Sawyer was in the lead.

When she slammed her foot on the brake, the Jeep slid to a halt and the engine died.

Sawyer yanked open the door. "Scoot," he ordered.

Jenna crawled across the console into the passenger seat while Montana and Duff dived into the backseat.

Sawyer had the car in gear and moving before the doors closed.

Sirens wailed, the sound coming through the broken back window.

Without a word, Sawyer zigzagged through the narrow streets, angling away from the resort.

Jenna gripped the armrest, her body shaking, her breathing ragged.

When the sirens faded away, Sawyer turned back, taking the long way around, but eventually returning to the resort. Finally he turned toward Jenna. "Where's the gun?"

Her eyes widened. For a moment she couldn't remember. Then she became aware of the hard lump under her. She fished the nine-millimeter pistol from beneath her and held it out.

Sawyer pressed his hand against the side of the weapon, pointing it toward the front of the vehicle instead of his head. "Remind me to teach you how to use one of these."

"I shot him," she said.

"Who did you shoot?"

She jerked her head toward the broken window. "The man who broke the window. There were four of them, and waving an empty gun didn't impress them one bit." Jenna glared at Sawyer. "I could have been killed."

Sawyer reached out and took her hand. "You're right. I should have left the bullets in it."

Still frowning, she gripped his hand and held on until he had to free himself to shift into a lower gear at a traffic light.

Duff leaned forward. "Did you kill the guy?"

She shook her head. "I don't think so. I shot him in the leg. When his friends dragged him away, he was still conscious and cursing."

Montana chuckled. "I'd take her on my team anytime."

Sawyer shifted gears and pulled through the intersection, taking her hand again. "I'm sorry. Leaving you alone was a bad idea."

Jenna squeezed his hand. "I was the one who insisted on coming along. And besides, I survived." Now that she wasn't shaking, she could think straight. She'd managed to defend herself and survive. But it could have turned out so much worse. Perhaps Sawyer had been right. Maybe she should have stayed behind. "Did you question Ramirez?"

"We did."

"And? Did he tell you where to find Devita?"

Sawyer shook his head. "Not exactly."

Jenna stared at Sawyer's profile as he pulled into the resort parking lot. "What do you mean?"

Duff chuckled. "We planted a tracking device on him."

"Lance should be picking him up," Montana added. "Ideally, he'll take us right to Devita."

"Then why are we going back to the resort?"

Sawyer's lips pressed into a straight line. "To grab the handheld tracker and to drop you off with Lance. Going into Devita's compound will be a lot more dangerous than wading into the dark side of Cancún to catch Ramirez. And despite shooting a guy in the leg at point-blank range, you don't have the combat training or experience."

"But—"

Sawyer pulled to a halt between two other vehicles and faced her. "Jenna, you'll slow us down. Which puts my guys at risk."

Her gut clenched. God, she'd been selfish. Her lack of training and experience could cost the lives of these fine men. "I understand. But remember, the man who hired these people doesn't care whether you're brought in dead or alive."

"I've been in tougher situations." He gave her a gentle

smile. "Situations in which the people I went up against didn't have a choice. Kill me or be killed. At least with these people, I have a fifty-fifty chance." He winked.

She was sure he had been in tougher circumstances. But she hadn't known him then. Now that she did, she felt connected, as if she had a stake in his life. She wanted him around so that she could get to know him better. And if she wasn't careful, she might even fall in love with the SEAL.

Butterflies fluttered in her belly, and her cheeks heated. *Damn.* Now was not the time to fall for anyone. She was fresh from a colossal jilting, and Sawyer had one of the most dangerous jobs in the world.

Unfortunately, she feared it was already too late.

SAWYER WOULD WAIT for only a few minutes. Now that it was broad daylight, he didn't dare walk to the back of the resort where the bungalows were. He'd be a sitting duck for the hired gun waiting to polish him off.

Montana had texted Lance to meet them in the front parking lot. He should be there any moment.

The sandy-haired SOS agent emerged from the side of the hotel building and jogged across the pavement, searching for them, his head craning, swiveling right and left. When he spotted the Jeep between the other two vehicles, he made a beeline for them, carrying a large satchel.

As he reached the Jeep, Sawyer got out and stood in the V of the open driver's door.

No sooner had he left the vehicle than something plinked against the metal door.

"What—" Jenna cried out.

"Get down!" Duff yelled.

Sawyer ducked back into the vehicle.

Duff opened his door and slid to the middle of the seat. "Get in, Lance!"

Lance dived in, landing in a heap across Montana and Duff's laps.

Sawyer didn't wait for the back door to close. He ripped the shift into Reverse and slammed his foot on the accelerator. The Jeep shot out of the parking space and stayed in Reverse until they reached the road. More bullets pelted the exterior, several hit the windshield, blasting through the interior. Then Sawyer twisted the steering wheel around, spinning the vehicle in the road, and sped away from the resort high-rise.

"Do we have what we need?" Sawyer asked.

"If we don't, it's too bad." Lance righted himself and pulled the satchel off his shoulder. "You can't go back to the resort."

Sawyer snorted. "I sure as hell can't take you and Jenna to confront Devita."

"And we need Quentin in on this operation," Duff pointed out. "Anyone seen him lately?"

"After you left this morning, he and Jenna's roommate stopped by to see if they could help with anything. He told me to let you know that he and Carly will be at the marina, checking out all the boats, but ready for anything. All you have to do is say the word."

"Good. We need him now." Sawyer turned the Jeep toward the marina.

Duff called Quentin's cell phone number and barked, "We'll be there in five." When he ended the call, he said, "Quentin's ready."

Sawyer pulled into the marina and parked. His gaze slid over Jenna's chalk-white face. To the men in the backseat he said, "This works out perfectly. While we follow Ramirez, Lance and the ladies should be fine on the boat."

"I'll have Natalie join them for additional protection."

Duff's lips curled. "She hasn't been too happy about being left out of all the action."

Montana laughed. "I would have thought she got all the action she wanted when she put herself out there to be sold into the sex trade."

Duff's lips thinned. "That was a close call. I truly believe she would have found a way out, even without our help. She's that kind of tough."

"Call her," Sawyer said. "I'd feel better knowing Lance has some help protecting Jenna and her friend."

"I can take care of myself." Jenna held up the nine-millimeter pistol, which wobbled in her hand.

"Hey." Sawyer grabbed for it and shoved the muzzle toward the front of the vehicle. "Watch where you're pointing that thing."

Jenna's cheeks suffused with color, making her even more adorable. Sawyer wanted to end this chase and kiss this woman who'd risked her life to save his.

Duff called Natalie and passed on the information she needed. "She'll be here in less than fifteen minutes. She's coming from the airport, after seeing her sister onto her flight back to the States." Duff shook his head, a grin spreading across his face. "She says she's up for some adventure."

Sawyer glanced at the look on Duff's face, envying him for having found a woman who was his equal, someone with whom he could potentially spend the rest of his life. And he'd found her in a matter of a couple of days in Cancún.

Frowning, Sawyer nodded to the rest. "Let's get to the boat and make a plan. We don't have much time. If Ramirez really doesn't know where to find Devita, we'll need to follow his contact. And that contact will not have a tracking device."

The men piled out of the Jeep.

Sawyer rounded the vehicle to open Jenna's door, but she'd already gotten down.

She touched his arm and stared up into his face. "You don't have to provide protection for me. I'm not the one they're after."

"But you were the one who took the case and you've already been attacked once. The gunman might come back, looking for the case and you."

"I have it hidden back at the resort," Lance said. "It's in the rafters of the bungalow. Unless someone is looking straight at it, they won't find the case."

"Good to know." Sawyer gave Lance half a smile. "That's one less gun aimed at my head." He caught Jenna's hand and led the way along the dock to the slip where the yacht was moored.

Jenna's eyes rounded, and she laughed. "This isn't a boat. It's a yacht. Is it yours?"

Quentin, Montana and Duff all laughed as one.

"We wish," Quentin said. He helped Carly into the boat and entered the glassed-in lounge area, his arm around her, all the way.

Sawyer didn't join in the humor. His father had a yacht he kept moored at the Capital Yacht Club in the DC area. His teammates didn't know that. Hell, only Duff knew Sawyer's father was US Senator Rand Houston, a self-made millionaire who'd clawed his way to a huge fortune in the oil and gas industry.

When Sawyer was growing up, his father never spent more than three days a month at home with his family. Vacations were interrupted or short-lived for the man. When he'd turned to politics, Sawyer had seen even less of his father. But by then, he didn't care. As soon as he'd graduated from college, he joined the navy and applied for the

SEALs, as different and far away from his father's life as he could get.

Of course, his father had been disappointed—no, he'd been livid at his son's choices. He'd planned on Sawyer taking over the business and following in his footsteps.

"What's wrong?" Jenna pulled Sawyer to a halt before following the others into the lounge.

Sawyer frowned. "Besides being the target of a mad gunman? I can't think of a thing. Why do you ask?"

"You frowned when everyone else laughed." She pulled her hand free. "I don't want to be a burden to you or your team. I should probably go. I can always see if Carly and I can catch an early flight home."

Sawyer hated that his thoughts regarding his father had turned his expression sour. He didn't like Jenna feeling as though he didn't want her there. "In the meantime, where would you go? And if the gunman thinks you and I are in any way connected, he might still come after you to get to me."

She ran her tongue across her bottom lip, making Sawyer all kinds of crazy. "I've put you in a bind, haven't I?"

He gripped her arms and stared down into her eyes. "You saved my life. The least I can do is make sure you're not in danger."

She laughed and pushed a strand of her hair behind her ear. "It gets complicated, doesn't it?" The hair refused to stay and fell in her face.

He brushed the lock of hair back, tucking it behind her ear again, his knuckles skimming her jaw as he drew his hand away. He ached with the need to kiss her.

"Okay, I've got him on the screen," Lance said from inside. "Sawyer, you want to see this?"

"Yeah." Sawyer cupped Jenna's cheek. "Whatever you might think, you're not a burden. And I'm really glad you hijacked my WaveRunner." He winked and pulled her into the lounge with him.

Lance had a laptop computer set out on a tabletop with a map of the city of Cancún displayed. In the center, a dot blinked bright green, moving along a boulevard to the east. Lance pointed at the dot. "That's Ramirez. He's still on the move."

"That's good news." Sawyer glanced at his fellow SEALs. "You ready to find Devita?"

"Hell, yeah!" Montana, Quentin and Duff all answered as one.

"You'll need these." Lance dug in his satchel and pulled out a handheld two-way radio, several headsets and a handheld tracking device. "I can keep tabs on Ramirez from here and give you directions if the handheld device fails you. Find the weapons you need in the arsenal below and get out there before Ramirez stops."

While the men hurried below, Jenna moved to Lance's side. "Why do they have to catch up with Ramirez before he stops?"

"When he stops, most likely he'll be meeting with Devita's contact. We don't have a tracker on the contact, and he's the guy we'll need to lead us to Devita."

Jenna nodded.

Carly stepped beside Jenna. "Why didn't you tell me you were in trouble?"

Jenna snorted softly. "You were otherwise occupied. Besides, I'm not the one in trouble." She tilted her head toward the stairs leading down into the bowels of the yacht. "Sawyer's the one who is in trouble."

"Yeah, but Quentin tells me you found a sniper's rifle in that case you picked up by mistake in the lobby. The sniper could turn on you to collect that case." Carly slipped an arm around Jenna's waist. "Sweetie, when you said you wanted a more adventurous life, I thought zip-lining was pushing the envelope." She laughed. "This is above and beyond proving to your ex that you are nowhere near boring."

Jenna watched the stairs, waiting for the men to reappear. "I think we could all use a little boredom right now." Her heart flipped and fell to the pit of her belly when Quentin climbed the stairs carrying a small machine gun.

Montana followed with a similar weapon and a pistol. Duff was next with a rifle and a pistol.

Finally Sawyer appeared, dressed in jeans, a dark T-shirt and black tennis shoes. He held a rifle and a handgun. "Ready?" he asked the others.

"Let's do this," the men said in unison.

They loaded the larger weapons into a duffel bag and tucked the pistols into the waistbands of their trousers.

Sawyer stopped in front of Jenna. "Please, stay here until we get back."

She nodded, knowing now wasn't the time to argue. They might be about to confront the head of a dangerous drug cartel. Sawyer didn't need any distractions to keep him from his goal. If Devita was at the root of the kidnappings or this assassination attempt, Sawyer needed to know why.

Was Devita acting on his own, expecting to collect some ransom? Or was he being paid to take Sawyer out of commission by someone else?

Jenna wished with all her heart she could go with the men. Not knowing what was happening or if they would even return unharmed would kill her.

Before Sawyer turned to leave, she grabbed for his arm, leaned up on her toes and brushed his mouth in a brief but heartfelt kiss.

His arm came around her, and he crushed her body to

his, deepening the kiss, his mouth firm and insistent. Then he let go and was gone.

Jenna ran outside onto the deck as the SEALs marched across the dock and out to the damaged Jeep in the parking lot. When she could see them no more, she still stood staring at the empty street.

"Sweetie." Carly's arm circled her, and she pulled Jenna close. "You might as well come inside. The fewer people who see you, the less your chance of being discovered here."

Jenna allowed Carly to lead her into the luxurious lounge, where Lance remained glued to the laptop monitor, his hand on the two-way radio, the device held close to his mouth. "Turn left at the next street. It appears to be a shortcut."

Jenna paced, pausing several times to glance at the green blip on the screen.

Ten minutes after the men left, a tall, beautiful blond-haired woman came aboard the yacht.

Lance glanced her way and smiled. "Natalie. Glad you could make it." He tipped his head toward Jenna. "Jenna and Carly are friends of Sawyer and Quentin."

Natalie smiled and held out her hand to shake hands with Jenna and Carly. "Nice to meet you." Then she turned to Lance, her expression all business. "You want to fill me in on what's going on?"

In a few short minutes, Lance told Natalie what was happening with the SEALs.

She frowned. "Do they know what they're up against? Devita is one of the most notorious kingpins of the primary drug cartel in the Cancún area. He probably has an army of bodyguards surrounding him at all times. How in hell do they expect to reach him without getting themselves killed?"

Jenna's chest clenched. She'd had similar thoughts, having read all about Mexico's troubles with cartels running the country. She stepped up to Natalie. "There has to be another way to find out who is after Sawyer."

Natalie's lips firmed, and she glanced at Lance. "How involved is Royce in this investigation?"

"Very. He assigned me to help while he's checking his connections."

"Why Sawyer?"

Lance clicked on the touch pad, bringing up a blank screen. His fingers flew over the keypad and finally brought up an image of Sawyer Houston in his navy uniform, along with all his personal data. He zoomed in on his next of kin and pointed. "That would be my guess."

"What?" Jenna leaned over Lance's shoulder, squinting to see the small print on the monitor.

"His father is Rand Houston."

Jenna straightened. "Rand Houston? As in Senator Rand Houston?"

Natalie let out a low whistle. "A senator's son makes a lot of sense for a kidnapping and ransom. But why kill him?"

Lance shook his head. "Perhaps the good senator has some enemies who are trying to make a point."

"Does Royce know this?"

Lance shook his head. "He hasn't said anything to me about being the son of a senator."

"Wow." Jenna ran a hand through her hair. "I wonder if the senator knows his son is being targeted."

"I don't think Sawyer has contact with his father. From what I can tell, his teammates don't know he's Senator Houston's son. He doesn't advertise the fact that he was born with a silver spoon in his mouth."

Jenna would never have guessed. Sawyer seemed to be

an equal among the members of his team, not better than anyone and willing to put his life on the line for them.

Her heart swelled at that kind of commitment. To have friends willing to do anything for you... What a concept. Unlike her former friend who'd been having an affair with her fiancé behind her back while helping her plan a wedding that would never be.

"Wow," Carly said. "Who'd have thought that when you jumped on the back of a WaveRunner, you'd be saving the life of a senator's son?"

Whether or not he was the son of a rich and highly influential politician didn't matter to Jenna. Who his father was didn't make Sawyer the man he was. Sawyer was who he was because he'd done it on his own. Nobody could buy his way onto one of the navy's elite SEAL teams.

Lance switched back to the tracking screen and lifted the two-way radio. "Where are you now?"

A blast of static was followed by the names of two streets at an intersection.

"You're two blocks from Ramirez and he has stopped. You better hurry if you're going to catch him. You have to be there to follow Devita's contact if he doesn't trust Ramirez."

"On it."

Jenna's heart thumped against her ribs and she held her breath, waiting to hear something. Anything that indicated the men had found the man they were looking for, and that they'd come out of it alive.

The thought of waiting for hours on the boat, not knowing if they lived or died, was unbearable. But where else would she go? At least here with Lance she might hear something sooner. So she stayed put and waited, her pulse pounding in her ears.

Chapter Nine

Sawyer muscled the steering wheel, taking the corners at breakneck speeds, sending the Jeep sliding sideways several times.

His teammates kept their comments to themselves, gripping the handles located above each door. Duff sat shotgun, the handheld tracking device in front of him. Quentin had responsibility for maintaining communications with the two-way radio in the backseat.

Static erupted from the radio, followed by Lance's tinny voice. "Turn left at the next corner."

Jamming his foot to the brake pedal, Sawyer skidded around the next corner, then hit the accelerator and straightened the vehicle.

Duff glanced up and barked, "Kid chasing a dog."

Once again, Sawyer slammed on his brakes, let the kid and dog pass, then hit the gas.

"Ramirez has stopped," Duff said.

"How far?" Sawyer demanded.

Duff glanced at the tracking device. "Two blocks, parallel to our position. Drop me at the next alley. I'll go on foot to spot the vehicle."

"I'll go. Montana, get ready to drive. Headsets on." Sawyer touched the on switch for the headset he had already embedded in his ear. As he came to an alley, he shifted the Jeep into Park, grabbed the tracking device and leaped out of the Jeep.

Montana was out and into the driver's seat before Sawyer entered the alley between run-down buildings and stucco walls.

The display not only indicated where Ramirez was but also gave Sawyer the location of the tracking device Sawyer held in his hand. He was quickly closing the distance between himself and Ramirez.

At the end of the alley, he glanced both ways before crossing a dingy, deserted street and entering another alley between older, derelict buildings covered in faded advertisements and graffiti. As he neared the street where Ramirez had stopped, he slowed and halted at the corner.

Crouching low, he eased forward to peer around the side of the building in the direction Ramirez had stopped.

A dark four-door sedan sat at the side of the street. Alone.

Sawyer studied the vehicle. The darkened windows gave no clue to how many men were inside. The steady blip on the screen reassured him Ramirez was one of them.

"What do you see?" Duff asked, his tone tight.

"One vehicle sitting. Nothing moving."

The squeal of tires on pavement alerted Sawyer. "Got company."

A large black SUV careened around the corner, coming fast.

Sawyer backed into the shadow of the building until the vehicle screeched to a stop behind the sedan.

Four heavily armed thugs climbed out of the SUV, aiming their weapons at the sedan. One shouted in Spanish for the occupants of the vehicle to get out.

Ramirez stepped out of the passenger door, his hands

held high, a pistol dangling from one finger. The driver slid out and straightened slowly, his eyes wide.

Ramirez spoke so fast, Sawyer couldn't make out all the words. He picked out mention of Devita, the word for *woman* and then the words for *son*, *senator* and *Houston*. In the heat of the day, a cold chill settled over his body.

After speaking sharply, the leader of the four men turned away, motioning to his men to follow.

Before they'd taken one step toward the SUV, a shot rang out. Ramirez's guayabera blossomed with a bright red splash of blood, and he fell to the ground.

What the hell?

Sawyer glanced down the street in the direction the bullet had to have come from.

The leader of the group dived for the SUV. His men followed suit. Once inside, he lowered a window, pointing his submachine gun everywhere he looked. When he turned toward the alley where Sawyer stood, his eyes narrowed, and he paused.

Sawyer froze, praying the bright sun in the street made the shadows where he stood dark enough to conceal him.

Ramirez's driver flung himself into his vehicle and burned a layer of rubber off his tires in an attempt to get away as quickly as possible.

"I heard a gunshot. What's happening?" Quentin asked.

Sawyer didn't respond, not willing to move his lips, whisper or even bat an eyelash until the men moved on.

The SUV jerked forward, raced to the end of the street and squealed around the corner.

"I'm all right," Sawyer finally responded. "Devita's contacts came and left. Someone shot Ramirez, but it wasn't Devita's contact. The contact is on the move, heading east."

"On our way," Quentin said. "Meet you one block east

of Ramirez's last position. And for Pete's sake, keep your head down!"

Sawyer remained in the shadows until the SUV sped away and turned left at the end of the street. As soon as the vehicle was out of sight, Sawyer sprang to his feet, backed down the street cut through an alley and arrived as the Jeep slid to a halt.

"Turn right." Sawyer jumped into the backseat and yelled, "Go! Go! Go!"

Before the door closed, Montana yanked the steering wheel to the right and hit the accelerator, shooting the Jeep forward. Sawyer nearly fell out during the turn and then slammed back against the seat, the door shutting automatically with the blast of forward motion. "Left at the end of the street." He leaned forward, peering between the seats at the road ahead.

"What happened back there?" Duff asked.

"Apparently, Ramirez was informing Devita's contact what had transpired. I didn't catch everything they said before the shooting started. *Devita*, *woman* and *Houston* were what I got out of it." He didn't mention he'd heard the words *son of a senator*. Sawyer wanted to check out that angle on his own before he brought it up to his teammates. "Someone fired a shot at Ramirez."

"Who?" Duff asked.

"Not Devita's contact or his men," Sawyer said. "They were just as surprised as I was."

Montana snorted. "Great. I'll bet it was your gunman." He whipped the steering wheel to the left at the corner the SUV had taken a minute before.

Sawyer's heart skipped several beats when he didn't see the SUV. "What the hell?"

"Had to have turned." Montana raced down the street, slowing at every crossroad.

"There!" Duff pointed to the right at one of the narrow streets they passed.

Montana slammed on the brakes, shoved the gear stick into Reverse, backed up, turned and hit the gas.

The SUV was three blocks ahead, turning left on another road, moving fast.

"Don't get too close. We can't spook them," Sawyer warned. "We need to find Devita."

"We won't get to Devita if we lose that SUV," Montana said, flooring the accelerator.

At the corner where the SUV had turned, Montana barely slowed as he entered an area with several large, abandoned warehouse buildings. They couldn't see around the corner until they turned and it was too late.

The SUV stood sideways in the middle of the narrow road, blocking it completely, the four men inside climbing out with their weapons held at the ready.

Montana slammed on the brakes, throwing Sawyer forward. He hit the back of the driver's seat, momentarily stunned. Then he dived for one of the loaded submachine guns on the floor. "Duck!" Sawyer yelled.

All four SEALs ducked in their seats as the cartel thugs opened fire on the Jeep. Bullets peppered the hood and blew through the windshield.

Montana shifted into Reverse and backed out of the street, unable to look behind him.

Sawyer prayed they didn't hit a building before they got out of range of the bullets pelting the front end of the Jeep. One must have hit the radiator, because steam spewed from beneath the hood.

Sawyer hit the button to lower the window. When it was down, he leaned out, pointing the submachine gun at Devita's men, letting loose a stream of bullets. They ran behind the relative safety of the SUV, buying the SEALs enough time for Montana to swerve backward around the corner and out of sight of the cartel thugs.

Montana whipped the Jeep around and sped away.

"What are you doing?" Sawyer turned to look behind him. "We need to follow them."

"This mission is over. They won't lead us to Devita now. If anything, they'd lead us to a bigger ambush than we just experienced," Duff reasoned.

"Besides, the Jeep might not last until we get back to the marina." Montana drove the Jeep full throttle to get them as far away from the SUV and Devita's men. "The water in the radiator is leaking fast. Either the engine will burn up or other damage will bring us to a halt before we get back."

Sawyer and Quentin kept a close eye on their rear in case the men from the SUV came after them. When they were certain they weren't being followed, they settled back in their seats.

"Everyone all right?" Sawyer asked.

"I'm good," Montana responded.

"Good here," Quentin said beside Sawyer.

"Duff?" Sawyer prompted.

For a moment he didn't respond. Finally he said through gritted teeth, "I'll be fine when we can get back and put a plug in the hole I have in my right arm."

Quentin handed Sawyer the radio equipment and leaned forward to check the wound. "The good news is that the bullet went clean through and lodged in the back of your seat." His lips twisted. "Lucky for me. Otherwise it would have hit me in the head. The bad news is, you're bleeding like a stuck pig."

Sawyer laid the radio in his lap and yanked his T-shirt over his head. "Here." He handed the shirt to Quentin, who used it to apply pressure to the wound and stem the flow of blood.

"We should get him to a hospital," Sawyer said.

"Hell, no," Duff muttered. "We'd have the Mexican police all over us in two seconds flat. We can't go to the hospital or the police. Not with a Jeep full of bullets and guns. And if Devita has control of the local government, we'd be playing right into their hands."

"Good point." Quentin grinned. "Guess you'll have to let one of *us* sew you up."

"It sure as hell won't be you," Duff mumbled.

Sawyer lifted the handheld radio to let Lance know they were coming in. "We have one wounded. See what you can find on the yacht that we can use to patch someone up."

When Jenna heard the call come through on the radio, she recognized Sawyer's voice immediately and breathed in a deep lungful of air for the first time in the thirty minutes the men had been gone. When he mentioned someone had been injured, her chest pinched tight, and she was right back to being worried. Was it Sawyer? Had he called in and played it off like it was nothing? Or was it one of the teammates he cared so deeply about?

Natalie's lips pressed together as she responded. "Roger." When she turned to face Carly and Jenna, she stared hard at them. "Either of you good at first aid?"

Carly raised her hand. "I'm a nurse."

Natalie let go of a long breath. "Good. I'll get the first-aid kit."

"I'll get towels and cloths to clean the wound." Jenna scrambled down the stairs into the lower level of the yacht. She opened doors, locating what appeared to be a store-room for scuba gear and fishing equipment. A panel in one of the walls jutted out from the others. When she neared it, she realized it was a hidden door to another room. When she stepped inside, she gasped.

From floor to ceiling, the room was filled with weapons of all kinds. This must have been where the men found their machine guns, rifles and pistols. And there were more than any normal yacht owner could possibly use by himself for protection.

Who owned the yacht? And how were the SEALs connected to that owner? From what Jenna had gathered, Lance wasn't a SEAL or in the military. Neither was Natalie, but they knew what the equipment was and how to use it.

Jenna ran her hand over one of the rifles, caressing the long, sleek barrel. It was cool against her fingertips. What was it like to be in a shoot-out? Hell, was it even called a shoot-out? Was this the kind of life Sawyer led on a daily basis? One filled with danger, the possibility of being shot—or worse, coming home in a body bag?

She flinched away from the rifle and pressed her hand against her belly where her stomach knotted. What kind of life was it for the women who loved men who put their lives on the line every day?

If something ever developed between her and Sawyer, could she see herself sitting at home, waiting to hear if he was dead or alive? Then again, people died every day in automobile wrecks. Who was to say she wouldn't be the one to die first?

She left the arsenal and found a linen closet filled with sheets, towels and cloths. With her pulse pounding, Jenna grabbed a couple towels and washcloths, and then shot up the stairs and through the lounge as the four SEALs boarded the yacht. Her gaze went immediately to Sawyer, skimming his body for any sign of injury.

Natalie rushed toward Duff and slipped her hand around his waist, allowing him to drape his arm over her shoulder. "Figures you'd be the one to take a bullet." She shook her head, her lips held in a tight smile that didn't reach her eyes. "You're in luck today. We have a nurse on board."

"Oh, yeah?" He glanced around. "Where?"

"That would be me." Carly carried the first-aid kit to a table and pointed to a chair. "Sit."

"I don't know which is worse, getting shot or taking orders from bossy women." He winked and did as he was told.

Natalie held out her hand. "Knife."

Quentin and Montana pulled their knives out of the scabbards on their hips.

Rolling her eyes, Natalie selected the one closest to her and turned to Duff.

His eyes widened. "It's only a flesh wound."

Quentin backed him up. "The bullet went clean through."

Natalie chuckled. "Relax, I'm only going to cut away the shirt." She shook her head. "What did you think? That I was going to go all Clint Eastwood and dig the bullet out?"

Quentin, Duff and Montana all exchanged sheepish grins.

Natalie snagged the shirtsleeve with the tip of the knife and yanked it up, ripping the sleeve away from his arm and exposing the wound. Still holding the knife, she nodded toward Carly. "Your turn."

Carly eyed the knife and the woman. "You sure you're not going to use that knife on anything else?"

Natalie laughed. "Do I look like that much of a badass?"

Carly and Jenna nodded and answered as one. "Yes."

Duff glanced up at Natalie. "It wasn't just me." And he winked, reaching out to pat her bottom.

"I'll leave Carly to it, then." Natalie handed the knife to Quentin and walked away. "Silly men."

Jenna only half listened to the banter, her gaze following Sawyer as he paced the interior of the lounge. A deep frown creased his forehead, and he kept looking at Duff's injured arm. Finally he spun toward the stairs and descended to the lower level of the yacht.

Jenna hesitated at the top of the stairs before going down.

She located him by the harsh sound of his voice, talking fast and angry.

He'd gone into the storage room with the hidden arsenal, leaving the door slightly ajar.

"Get him on the phone now. Tell him it's an emergency. I don't care if he's with the president himself. Do it!" A few moments of silence stretched by.

Jenna decided to let him know she was there and had just reached for the door to open it wider when Sawyer spoke again.

"What the hell did you do?"

For a moment Jenna thought he was talking to her, but he had his back to her, his phone pressed to his ear, his body rigid.

"Don't even pretend to be ignorant. I'm on my damn vacation with a couple of my teammates in Cancún, and I'm getting shot at. When I chase down some of the drug cartel to find out who's responsible, I overhear them talking about Senator Houston's son. Ringing any bells yet? Did you get on the wrong side of a drug cartel in Mexico? Because if you did, you'd better let me know now. One of my guys took a bullet today. And an innocent woman is now being targeted, as well. If she or any of my men are seriously injured or killed, I swear I'll…"

Jenna's cheeks warmed at his mention of her. Guilt at eavesdropping forced her to take a step backward. She could wait to talk to Sawyer after he'd finished his call. Clearly, he'd gone below to complete the call in private.

She took another step backward, her heel catching on something. Jenna teetered and lost her balance, her arms flailing as she fell over a scuba tank, toppling it and the one beside it, making a loud metal clanging sound.

Sawyer threw open the door and glared down at her. To the person on the other end of the conversation, he said, "Great. Just what I wanted to hear. I'll be in touch once I nail the bastard trying to kill me. And mark my words, I'll get to the bottom of this."

Sawyer hit the end button, reached for her hand and pulled her off the floor and into his arms. "How much of that did you hear?"

Her cheeks burned. "Enough."

He hugged her close, holding her tightly against him, crushing the air out of her lungs. For a long moment he held her this way.

Jenna wrapped her arms around his waist and told herself she didn't need to breathe as badly as Sawyer apparently needed to be held.

When she thought she might have to remind him she needed air, he finally loosened his hold and lifted his head to stare down into her eyes. "Duff took a bullet for me." He ran a hand through his hair, standing it on end. "Hell, any one of us could have been killed today. I asked myself why anyone would target me. I'm just a SEAL." He snorted. "Just goes to prove you can't leave your past behind when your past refuses to go away."

"This has to do with you being the son of Senator Houston." She didn't pose it as a question.

"You knew?"

Jenna shook her head. "Not until a little while ago when Lance pulled you up on a screen and showed us who you really are."

Sawyer frowned. "It's a shame kids can't choose their

parents. I wanted to be known for who I am, not for who my father is. He wasn't even a good father or role model. What I've done, I've earned on my own."

Jenna nodded. "I can't imagine the navy SEALs cutting any candidate slack, no matter who their parents are."

"Damn right. Either you make it on your own or you wash out."

"And you made it on your own," she said softly, glad he was sharing with her. His fierce expression told her he needed to vent more tension.

"But my father's life is still haunting me. Devita's men mentioned the son of a senator. They had to be talking about me. Frankly it's the only explanation for why I've been targeted and no one else has."

Jenna frowned. "I can understand bringing you in alive. The cartel could stand to make a lot of money off your ransom. But to kill you?" Jenna tightened her arms around his waist and leaned her head against his chest. "Why would they kill someone who could be lucrative to them?"

"It's easier to kill someone than to bring him in alive. If they were offered money to kill me, why take the time to kidnap me and hold me for ransom? My father is known for his stance on terrorism. He doesn't negotiate with terrorists. I'm sure he wouldn't even consider paying a ransom for a son he never gave a damn about."

Jenna glanced up at him. "Your father has to love you. Surely he would offer the money they would demand."

Sawyer's jaw tightened. "You don't know my father. He never got to know his only son. He wasn't there for my birth, my first baseball game or my high school graduation. The only times he spoke to me were to point out my faults and tell me how disappointed he was that I chose to enter the navy. And he was even more disapproving of my decision to train to be a SEAL."

Jenna didn't know how to respond to Sawyer's description of his father. Her own had been there for her throughout her life. He'd been there to walk her down the aisle and had been the one to hustle her out of the church so she could avoid the embarrassment of facing all those people who'd come for her wedding. He was the rock in her life, and she loved him dearly.

"Come on." His lips twisted into a frown. "I have to break it to the team that I'm not who they thought I was."

"Don't be so hard on yourself. You're the man they know now."

He kissed the tip of her nose. "Thanks. We really have to get past this mess. You deserve a better time than being stuck fighting a battle you didn't start."

She gave him a lopsided smile. "What would I do with my time in Cancún? There's only so much sun a girl can absorb before she's completely sunburned and stuck inside, bored beyond redemption." Jenna squeezed his hand. "And the thing is, I'm not bored."

"Nor are you boring." Taking her hand in his, he led her up the stairs into the lounge. "Guys, I have something to say."

Duff pushed to his feet, his arm bandaged neatly. "You finally gonna tell everyone who the hell you are?"

Sawyer nodded.

Quentin and Montana looked on expectantly.

"You all might have heard of US Senator Rand Houston."

Montana nodded. "Sure. He's your father."

"Yeah," Quentin said. "But we never held it against you. You can handle an M4A1 like nobody's business."

Sawyer's fingers loosened on Jenna's hand. "You knew?"

Quentin shared a glance with Montana and then Duff.

"Sure. Every man on the team knows. So? What difference does it make?"

Jenna tried hard not to smile. She could feel Sawyer's relief in the way he held her hand. Her heart swelled for the love these men had for each other. What a great team to be a part of.

Sawyer pushed his shoulders back. "What difference it makes is that whoever is after me wants me because I'm the senator's son."

Chapter Ten

In the yacht's vault arsenal, Sawyer dismantled the submachine gun he'd used earlier, to clean it in preparation for the next operation. He found that working with his hands was therapeutic.

After a while, Duff entered with his hand pressed to the bandages on his arm. "You all right, buddy?"

"I'm fine." Sawyer ran a cloth over the barrel.

"I told you it was a flesh wound." Duff picked up the bolt and a soft cotton cloth and began rubbing oil into the metal.

Sawyer snorted. "I can't believe everyone knew who my father was and didn't let on."

Duff shrugged. "Wasn't important."

"Seems pretty important now. While you three should be enjoying a much-deserved vacation, you're getting shot at and chased by killers."

Duff smiled. "A typical day in the lives of us SEALs, wouldn't you say?" He handed the cleaned bolt back to Sawyer.

Sawyer inserted the bolt into the gun, fit the retainer pin and finished reassembling. When he had the weapon complete, he set it on the counter. "None of you should have to deal with my problems."

Duff's eyes narrowed. "Are you saying we aren't good enough to cover your six?"

"No, hell no. You're the best. But this isn't your mission."

"Like hell it's not. If one of us were targeted by a killer, you would have our backs. It's no different."

"But none of you are sons of a senator. Because I am, I bring an unnecessary element of risk to the team."

"And if I were to piss off a terrorist, and that terrorist decided he wanted revenge, you and the rest of the team wouldn't desert me because I was the only one targeted by the terrorist. You'd stand and fight with me." Again Duff shook his head. "You aren't alone in this. No matter what reason this killer has to place you in his crosshairs, you're one of us. We've got your back."

Sawyer faced his friend. This man had been through everything with him. From BUD/S training to multiple missions all over the world in some of the most dangerous, godforsaken situations.

Duff stuck out his hand. "We're in this together. Like it or not."

"Thanks." Sawyer grasped his forearm and pulled him into a quick hug.

"You two wanna join us up here?" Quentin called down the stairs.

Duff turned and led the way out of the arsenal and up to the lounge.

Sawyer followed, his heart swelling with the knowledge he had the best friends in the world. Friends who were the family he'd never had.

Everyone was gathered in the lounge.

Sawyer's gaze sought Jenna's. She returned his glance with a steady one of her own.

He took comfort in knowing she was there and safe.

Jenna and Carly stood on the periphery of the group gathered around Lance at his laptop. Sawyer joined them and leaned over the computer guru's shoulder to stare at the screen.

"My boss tapped into the CIA computers and found some information on Devita." Lance had a report pulled up and was skimming through it, the cursor moving along as he read. "Apparently Devita frequents a certain bar at one of the resort hotels, and he has a weakness for beautiful women."

"What bar?" Sawyer asked.

"It's at the Playa del Sol north of Cancún. He's a regular on Friday nights."

"What's today?" Sawyer asked. So much had happened, he'd lost track.

"Friday," Natalie supplied.

"Then let's go." Sawyer spun toward the door.

"Not so fast," Lance said. "This report says he takes a twenty-man contingent with him each time he goes. They check every man at the door and only allow women to enter unheeded."

"Sounds like you need me to get in," Natalie said.

Duff's brow dipped. "You aren't going in alone."

Jenna stepped forward. "I'll go."

"Me, too." Carly joined her friend. "What do we have to do?"

"All you would have to do is plant a tracking device on Devita," Lance said. "We can pinpoint his location without the ladies having to get any closer to the man."

"No way," Sawyer said.

"Agreed." Duff puffed out his chest. "The man has been known to deal in human trafficking. Three beautiful women might be too tempting a target for him to resist."

"It's a resort hotel," Jenna argued. "Surely they have

some security of their own to keep their guests safe from being kidnapped and sold into slavery. Otherwise, the trip reports would tag them as dangerous."

"Right," Carly added. "You heard Lance. All we have to do is get the tracking device into Devita's pocket. Then we can leave."

Irritated, Sawyer turned his attention back to Lance and the monitor. "Show me the map."

Lance brought up the map of the Yucatán Peninsula and pointed at the red dot that was the location of Playa del Sol.

Sawyer studied the image. "There's only one road in and out of that resort. They could easily set up a roadblock and take you ladies out."

"Then we go in by boat." Natalie pointed at the blue on the map. "It would probably be faster, anyway, and the shoreline provides a lot more room to maneuver should we be chased."

Sawyer glared at Jenna. "You've already done enough for me. I won't have you risking your life again."

She tilted her chin and smiled at him, making him want to grab and kiss her, despite her pigheadedness. "You don't have a choice. But I do. If I want to help, you can't stop me."

Sawyer turned to Natalie. "Don't take her."

Natalie patted Sawyer's cheek. "You can't give orders to us. We aren't in your military, sweetheart."

"Damn it!" Sawyer pounded his fist into his other palm. "Devita is a very dangerous man. Isn't anyone here at all concerned that Devita saw the same video we did and might recognize Jenna?"

Jenna nodded. "There is that possibility. I'll be sure to wear my hair and makeup differently so that I won't be as easily recognizable. Remember, Devita is also just a man who likes beautiful women." Her eyes narrowed. "Or are you saying I'm not beautiful and that I wouldn't have a chance to get close enough to plant a bug on him?"

Quentin laughed out loud. "Oh, Sawyer, your best bet is to walk away from that question. Any way you answer is going to get you in deeper than you already are."

Sawyer opened his mouth, thought about what Quentin said and snapped his mouth shut. He might as well argue with a rock. The women would not be dissuaded.

He took another tack. "Why don't we stage an assault on the bar while Devita is there? We could nab him and take him out without his men knowing."

Natalie shook her head. "He brings twenty men with him."

"We've had worse odds," Montana said.

"That twenty doesn't include the Mexican police and hotel security staff," Carly pointed out.

"Yeah, and why do it if you don't have to?" Jenna insisted.

"We'll be up against even more of his soldiers if we follow him back to his compound."

Natalie waved a hand. "You'd be up against his cartel minions. The Mexican government might be happy if you cleaned up a thorn in their side."

"Undoubtedly," Lance affirmed. "And staging an attack on his compound can be attributed to one of his rivals, whereas staging an attack on a public resort when there are so many other people besides Devita would be far too revealing to the public eye. You could cause an international incident."

Jenna touched Sawyer's arm. "Do you want to risk injuring innocent civilians at the Playa del Sol? What would your commander back home say if he found out, via the international news networks, that you have been conducting black ops?"

Montana chuckled. "She's good."

Cornered, Sawyer couldn't come up with another reasonable argument to deter the women from staging their own covert op. "I don't like it."

"You don't have to." Carly hooked her arm through Jenna's. "We'll be fine. We're just three reasonably attractive women, going for a night on the town at an upscale club. If we happen to attract the attention of a kingpin and drop a bug in his pocket...so be it." She winked at Quentin.

He laughed out loud. "I knew there was something I liked about you. You're not only a nurse but also a spy and a smart mouth? It's a killer combination." He took her hand and drew her into his arms. "I'd rather take you out dancing again than let you go out without me."

"There will be time." She leaned into him and faced the others. "Are we in?"

Outvoted and outmaneuvered, Sawyer was overrun.

"We need to get to our clothes back at the resort," Natalie noted.

"Quentin and I can take you," Duff offered.

"I'll go," Sawyer said.

"No, you need to stay here, out of range of the assassin, whom we have yet to identify."

"I don't give a damn about the assassin." Sawyer moved to follow the women to the door.

Duff stepped in front of him. "Two words. Collateral. Damage."

Sawyer stopped in his tracks, hating that Duff hit the nail on the head. He couldn't protect Jenna when it was his head that was being hunted. Whereas he trusted his own aim, he didn't trust a mercenary to hit him and not the woman standing beside him. "Fine. But let me know when you get there and when you leave."

"Roger." Duff hooked Natalie's elbow and ushered her toward the door. He paused, looking back at the men in the lounge. "Make sure we have what we need in the way of boats and weapons. The girls need us to be nearby in case all hell breaks loose."

"NICE," QUENTIN SAID as he entered before Carly and Jenna to check for intruders. Natalie brought up the rear carrying a gown she'd stopped to collect from her hotel on the way to Jenna's. "But this is the bridal suite." Quentin emerged from the bedroom, his brows raised. "Something you want to tell me?" And he winked.

"Not particularly." Jenna entered the suite and headed straight for the bedroom.

"It's a long story and we don't have time for it." Carly patted Quentin's face as she squeezed past him into the bedroom. "You can wait in the sitting area while we dress." She turned with her hand on the doorknob. "Help yourself to the champagne. Someone might as well enjoy it." Then she shut the door.

Jenna stood in the middle of the bedroom. Though it hadn't been long since she and Carly checked into the hotel, it felt like ages ago, and her entire life had been upended.

For a moment she wondered what would have happened if she'd never picked up that case in the lobby. Or if she'd decided to take a nap instead of going zip-lining with Carly that day. She might never have met Sawyer.

And Sawyer could very well be dead by now.

Jenna shivered.

"Are you going to get dressed?" Carly asked, her head in the closet.

"I was just thinking."

Carly emerged with two dresses. "About what?"

Jenna's lips quirked. "That zip-lining seems a breeze right now."

"Are you afraid of Devita?" Carly laid the dresses on the bed and crossed the room to her. "We don't have to do this."

Jenna shook her head. "I'm not letting Natalie go in there alone."

"I'm fine going in alone," Natalie said.

Jenna shook her head. "You need backup."

"Then stay here, and *I'll* go with her," Carly insisted.

"No way. I didn't bring you to Cancún with me to embroil you in a dangerous operation with drug cartel kingpins and assassination attempts."

"And you didn't come here to get yourself involved." Carly took her hands. "We can tell the guys we're out. That we don't want anything to do with this, and that they can walk away and leave us alone. We'll go back to being two women here on a relaxing vacation."

Jenna laughed out loud. "Do you hear yourself?"

"What?" Carly's brows furrowed.

"There is no going back to that relaxing vacation now. We're in this whether we like it or not." Jenna squeezed her friend's hands. "And the only way out of it is to find out who is after Sawyer and why, so we can nail the bastard and get on with our lives."

Carly's lips curled into a smile. "You like Sawyer, don't you?"

Jenna's cheeks heated. "I guess. I barely know him."

"I've only known Duff since I've been in Cancún," Natalie said, slipping her dress over her head. "And I can't imagine life without him now."

"So, Jenna, have you slept with Sawyer?" Carly asked.

Her face burning, Jenna glanced away.

"You have!" Carly whooped. "Good for you, Jenna.

Tyler didn't deserve you. He didn't take the time to get to know the strong and incredibly interesting woman you are."

"You're just saying that because you're my friend."

"No. I'm saying it because it's true." She hugged her and set her at arm's length. "And you're beautiful."

Jenna raised her hand to her head. "I have crazy hair."

"I'd give my right arm for that curl and color."

"Keep your arm. You might need it tonight." Jenna hugged her friend and stepped away. "Now, are we going to plant a bug on Devita or not?" She marched to the bed and lifted the sexy dress Carly insisted she buy as part of celebrating her freedom trip to Cancún.

"That's what I'm talking about. You've got more chutzpah than any woman I know. Let's do this. I'd have given my eyeteeth to see you jump on the back of Sawyer's WaveRunner. That's kickass, if you ask me."

Jenna shrugged. "Anyone would have done the same."

"You're wrong. Most folks would have taken that information straight to the Mexican police," Natalie said. "And they would have been too late."

Those had been Jenna's exact thoughts. And they were sobering. The women needed to get the bug on Devita and find out who had it in for Sawyer.

Fifteen minutes later, Jenna emerged from the bedroom garbed in a forest-green dress that hugged her body from her shoulders to her ankles. The neckline dropped almost down to her belly button in front. The back dipped to the lowest point in the small of her back without being considered indecent. The overall affect made her feel positively sexy and shameless.

Because they would be arriving by boat, she knew her hair would be a disaster if she left it down, so she'd pulled it up into a chic French twist, anchoring it with enough bobby pins to hold up against a typhoon-force wind. Carly helped her apply makeup to give her sexy, smoky eyes, emphasizing the deep green of her irises.

Shiny green emeralds sparkled at her throat and ears—a breakup gift to herself. On her feet she wore rhinestone-studded stilettos. She'd have to shed them to get on and off a boat, but to leave the hotel, she'd wear them like a champ, refusing to wobble.

A long, low wolf whistle sounded from near the windows. Quentin's face split in a wide grin. "Wow, Jenna. You look great."

Then Carly emerged wearing a shimmering golden dress that brought out the highlights in her bright cap of dark hair. Her dress emphasized the fullness of her breasts, her narrow waist and the sensuous swell of her hips.

Quentin issued another long, low whistle and held out his hands to Carly. "Wow."

"What?" She winked. "You talked my ear off all day and now you have nothing else to say but 'wow'?"

"You two are more beautiful than words can describe."

Carly tilted her head to the side. "That's better." She turned to Jenna. "Ready?"

Jenna's stomach quivered, on the verge of a full-scale panic attack.

Quentin waved a hand toward the door. "Sawyer called while you two were getting ready. They secured a couple of boats to take us to the Playa del Sol. I checked with Duff. He will pick us up out front. Everything is ready."

Just the mention of Sawyer strengthened Jenna's resolve. "Let's do this." She pushed her shoulders back and marched toward the door.

On the way down in the elevator, the door opened at the eighth floor and Becca Smith stepped in. Her eyes widened and swept Jenna, Natalie and Carly with an appreciative glance. "Wow, you three look amazing."

Jenna smiled. "Thank you. You look pretty great yourself."

Becca wore a long royal blue gown that hugged every curve to perfection, dipped to a deep V in the front and swooped low in the back. "Thank you. Are you going out?"

Jenna nodded.

The elevator stopped again and picked up two couples, all young and talking at once.

When they finally reached the lobby level, the couples piled out. Jenna stepped through after Becca. "Enjoy your evening," she said politely to the woman. Jenna's thoughts moved on to the task ahead.

Darkness had blanketed the Yucatán, the lights of the resort twinkling against the starlit sky. The ride to the marina took twenty minutes, the traffic slow as tourists hurried to make their dinner reservations at the many swanky restaurants and cafés.

Montana met them at the dock and led them to a different slip, where two small jet boats were moored. Sawyer straightened in the bow of one, his gaze going immediately to Jenna, his eyes widening. "Jenna?"

The shock and admiration shining from his eyes made Jenna even more confident in the choice of her dress.

He held out his hand. Instead of accepting it, she slipped out of her stilettos first, then took his hand and stepped off the dock into the boat. A small wave tipped the craft slightly as she set her foot onto the deck, and she lost her balance.

Sawyer yanked her into his arms, crushing her against his chest, holding her until she was steady on her feet.

Unfortunately, being so close to him made her even

less stable. Her knees wobbled, her pulse pounded and she couldn't quite catch her breath.

"Sweet heaven, you're beautiful," he said against her ear, the warmth of his breath sending shivers across her skin.

"Are you two going to make room for the rest of us?" Carly asked from above.

Jenna reluctantly pushed away from Sawyer, settled on a seat near the rear of the boat and wrapped a scarf around her hair.

Carly joined her and squeezed her knee. "I think he likes you, too."

Jenna didn't respond, her heart still racing and her breaths coming in short, ragged gasps. The man made her crazy with desire, and she was going to a club to seduce another man. She almost laughed out loud at the insanity of the evening ahead.

Quentin would drive the boat with the women, pretending to be the hired boat taxi driver, while the other three SEALs would tag along in the other boat in case they ran into trouble.

If all went as planned, the women would find Devita, plant the bug and leave shortly after. How hard could that be?

Jenna prayed it was as simple as that but suspected it wouldn't go off nearly as smoothly.

The water shimmered like glass, the tide and waves calm, making the ride around to the Playa del Sol smooth and uneventful. Jenna turned in her seat several times, looking for the other boat. Their craft sported the required lights affixed to the front and rear to make them easy to spot on the water. The boat carrying the other SEALs had the lights removed, making them harder to see and even harder to follow.

As they neared the dock at the Playa del Sol, Quentin slowed the boat.

Natalie sighed. "I wish I had my .40 caliber Heckler & Koch strapped to my leg beneath this dress."

"Honey," Carly said, "I don't think you could get anything else under that dress without it being real obvious."

Natalie laughed. "Exactly why we're going in unarmed. Besides, if one of Devita's men found a gun on us, there's no telling what would happen. Tonight we're just three women out for a good time."

"Do you have the tracking chip?" Jenna asked.

Natalie patted her breast. "I have it tucked into a tiny pocket inside the bra of this dress."

"I want the name of your seamstress," Carly said. "Why is it we never have pockets to carry important things?"

"Seriously," Natalie agreed.

Quentin shook his head. "It's a whole new world, taking women into a covert op."

Jenna chuckled nervously, praying she wouldn't unravel before they completed their mission.

Quentin pulled the boat into a slip at the dock, climbed out and helped the women alight.

"Break a leg," he whispered to Jenna as he assisted her onto the dock. Laying on a thick Spanish accent, he pointed to the resort hotel and said, "Follow boardwalk to hotel. I wait here for you."

Swallowing a giggle, Jenna slipped into her heels and trailed behind Carly and Natalie as they made their way along the boardwalk to the lavish hotel on the sand.

She hoped like hell she didn't break a leg, when she might need it to make a quick escape.

At the door, two armed men stopped them and demanded to see identification.

Jenna pulled her passport from the clutch she'd brought

along and showed it to one of the men. He stared at the picture and then her and finally nodded, waving his pistol for her to pass.

One hurdle overcome, they entered the building soon to be occupied by a drug cartel kingpin and his small army of thugs.

Chapter Eleven

"This is a mistake." Sawyer sat behind the steering wheel of the boat, watching from their position a hundred yards from the beach as the ladies crossed the boardwalk to the Playa del Sol.

"Three women at a bar on a Friday night shouldn't raise any red flags with Devita," Montana said.

"Yeah, but they shouldn't have to be there," Duff said. "We should be laying a trap for Devita and capturing him, not letting the women risk their lives to bug the guy."

"Four against twenty," Montana reminded him. "And civilians."

Sawyer's lips pressed together and his jaw tightened as the women disappeared from sight. "I don't like being this far out. Shouldn't we put in and observe from somewhere closer? If they need us, we could be right there."

"That was my plan," Duff nodded toward the beach farther along the strand. "Now that they are in, we can land on the beach and sneak up on the hotel."

"Now you're talking."

"Just remember not to engage unless it's absolutely necessary," Montana reminded them. "If bullets start flying, we put everyone in that building in danger."

"Got it." Sawyer patted the nine-millimeter pistol tucked into the waistband of his jeans as he shifted into

Forward and sent the little boat toward the shore farther along the beach, using the tide to ground the craft. Fortunately the tide was on its way out. They wouldn't have to worry about the craft being carried away if they left it for an hour.

Sawyer stepped out of the boat onto the sand and spoke into his headset. "The eagles have landed."

"The birds are in the cage," Quentin replied, indicating the ladies had entered the hotel.

Sawyer crossed the beach, aiming for the dunes and scrub brush. Moving from bush to bush, he made his way to the trunk of a palm tree at the edge of the hotel property. As they neared the hotel, the men split up. Montana took the corner of the hotel near the beach. Duff took the other corner, away from the beach. Sawyer slipped farther around the front, hoping to track Devita's movements into the hotel.

Two men wearing hotel security guard uniforms stood at the entrance, pistols seated in their holsters at their waists.

"Got a rear exit on this end," Montana reported. "And one security guard at the southwest corner."

"Another guard on the southeast corner," Duff's voice whispered into Sawyer's headset. "Want me to take him out?"

"Not yet. And only if necessary. Remember, we don't want an international incident."

"Gotcha," Montana responded. "Holding until you give the word."

"Same," Duff agreed.

Sawyer hid behind a bougainvillea bush, beneath a plumeria tree, lush with a plethora of blooms, the scent almost overpowering. He could see the circular drive leading to the hotel entrance from his position. So far, he'd seen no sign of Devita or his twenty-man army. For all they knew, the man would choose to skip his Friday-night routine and stay home. In which case it would be a long night waiting for a man who might not show.

Sawyer couldn't get over how amazing Jenna looked in that killer dress. His gut roiled at the thought of her being exposed to animals like Devita and his men. If anything happened, Sawyer and his teammates would get in somehow and get the ladies out, or die trying.

Five large, dark SUVs pulled into the circular drive, and men piled out carrying submachine guns and rifles. Some wore suits and ties. Others wore dark pants, T-shirts and black bandanas over their heads. The suits, carrying the automatic weapons, entered the hotel, blowing past the security guards, who didn't bother to draw their guns. Guests scurried out the front of the hotel, shooting worried glances over their shoulders.

The men dressed in black clothing spread out around the building, taking positions along the sides, standing guard with their automatic weapons at the ready.

Sawyer remained still, a couple of feet away from one of Devita's men.

When two suits came back out of the building, the driver of the middle SUV got out and walked around to the rear of the vehicle. He opened the door and held it while a man Sawyer recognized as Carmelo Devita stepped out, followed by another man—the one who'd been talking to Ramirez when Ramirez was shot in the street.

Sawyer's fists clenched. He didn't dare say a word into the mic, not with Devita's men so close. All he could do now was watch and wait for Devita to leave and take the tracking device with him. Preferably leaving the women behind.

Just knowing the gunman who'd shot Ramirez point-blank was inside with Jenna, Carly and Natalie made Sawyer's insides bunch.

His instincts were telling him this operation was a very bad idea.

JENNA, CARLY AND Natalie wandered through the hotel, following the sound of music from the big-band era.

Once again, they were stopped at the entrance to the bar and asked to show their passports to one guard while the other walked around them, eyeing them from head to toe, probably searching for any bulges in their dresses indicating they were packing guns.

Jenna's pulse galloped as they passed the test and were allowed to enter the barroom.

"Bar or table?" Carly asked, leading the way.

"Bar," Natalie replied. "I could use a drink."

Jenna scanned the room, searching for a man fitting the images of Devita that Lance had shown them on the computer earlier. So far, only a handful of people were scattered around some of the tables. Two older couples were swing dancing to the music the band played. A young couple sat at a table holding hands and drinking frozen concoctions from tall glasses topped with little umbrellas.

Natalie leaned toward Jenna and smiled. "He's not here yet. What's your poison?"

Jenna would have preferred a light beer, but seeing as how they were at an upscale bar, she said, "A mango vodka martini."

Carly gave her preference, and Natalie placed the order.

While they waited for their drinks, Jenna eased onto one of the bar stools, letting the slit in her skirt fall open, exposing much of her long legs, like she'd seen a seductress do in a movie.

God, she was playing way out of her league. How was

she going to convince Devita she was just a woman look-ing for a good time when she was shaking in her stilettoes?

The bartender set their drinks on the bar and turned to fill an order for one of the waitresses.

Natalie lifted a tumbler of what appeared to be whiskey into the air. "To good friends."

Carly lifted her chocolate martini, and all three women touched the rims of their glasses.

"To friends," Jenna said and drank a healthy swallow of alcohol, hoping it would calm her nerves without dull-ing them.

Before she could set her glass on the counter, four men entered the bar carrying guns and made a sweep of the en-tire room. Two of them stepped behind the bar and slipped into the storeroom beyond.

The bartender continued to mix drinks, acting as though the invasion was nothing out of the ordinary.

When the four men were satisfied, two left. The two remaining arranged tables and chairs at the back of the room to seat eight people.

A few minutes later, four guards entered with six men walking between them. The man in the middle walked with the air of someone who owned the place. Even in the dim lighting, Jenna could make out the arrogant features of Carmelo Devita, kingpin of the local drug cartel.

A shiver rippled down her spine. She turned toward Carly and Natalie, away from Devita, but watched him out of the corner of her eye.

"Let the party begin," she muttered beneath her breath and lifted her glass again to take a sip of the martini.

Natalie nodded, acknowledging she'd seen Devita, as well.

"So what is it you do, Jenna?" Natalie asked.

"I'm an accountant."

Natalie's lips turned up in a smile. "That's a tough job."

Jenna snorted softly. "I wouldn't say that. Actually, I'd say it's pretty boring."

"I used to have a desk job and worked near the nation's capital."

"What made you change careers?"

Natalie shrugged. "I got into my hobby and made a career out of it."

"What hobby?"

She lowered her voice and gave Jenna a crooked grin. "Marksmanship."

Carly lifted her glass to her lips and smiled. "Too bad we had to come in unarmed," she said, barely moving her mouth. She took a sip and set her glass on the bar.

Sitting sideways on the bar stool, Jenna could see the bartender quickly making a tray of drinks. A pretty, dark-haired, brown-eyed waitress stood at the counter, glancing nervously over her shoulder at the man and his henchmen sitting in the corner.

Finally the bartender nodded, and the waitress lifted the tray of drinks and hurried toward the drug lord.

After setting the drinks on the table, she lifted her empty tray and beat it back to the bar.

Devita lifted a tumbler of something that appeared to be whiskey to his lips and drank the entire glass in one gulp. Carefully setting the tumbler on the table, he scanned the room, his head turning as he observed every person, his gaze lingering on Jenna, Natalie and Carly.

Jenna's chest tightened. She couldn't let fear get the better of her. They were there to tag Devita with a tracking device. She lifted her martini glass and turned toward the dance floor, giving Devita the full impact of the ultralow back of her dress and the leg peeking out to the side of the slit. She drank another sip and set her glass on the bar.

She didn't know if he preferred blondes, brunettes or redheads. They had all three covered. He'd have his choice.

"Look out. Here comes our target," Natalie whispered, her head turned toward the dance floor but observing Devita in her peripheral vision.

"He's got his eye on Jenna," Carly said. "Pass the chip."

Natalie pretended to adjust the low-cut neckline of her dress, all the while slipping her fingers into the hidden pocket. She set the tiny disk on the bar and lifted her tumbler all in one smooth movement.

Out of the corner of her eye, Jenna could see Devita headed toward them, a man on each side, armed and wickedly dangerous.

Her heart thundering in her chest, Jenna reached for her martini, scooping up the disk before wrapping her fingers around the stem of her glass.

She smiled at the couples on the floor. "They're quite good," she remarked, though she couldn't have cared less about how well anyone in the room could dance.

A royal blue dress caught Jenna's attention, and she stared across the floor at Becca Smith sitting alone at a table at the far end of the barroom. What was she doing there alone? Before Jenna could comment, a hand touched her arm.

"Senorita, would you care to dance?" a heavily accented voice asked beside her.

Jenna turned toward Carmelo Devita, drug lord, human trafficker and killer, and shot him the best fake smile she could manage. "Me?" She touched her hand to her chest, the chip tucked beneath her thumb.

He nodded.

She batted her eyes and tried for shy when it was stark terror racing through her. "Oh, I don't know."

"Please," he said. "It would give me great pleasure, *mi armor*."

Jenna glanced at the other two.

Natalie nodded. "I'll save your seat at the bar. Go. Have fun."

With a smile at the two women, Jenna laid her hand in Devita's and slipped down from the stool. "Thank you. I love to dance."

Devita's hand was warm and slightly damp from perspiration. He took her hand in his and placed the other at the small of her back, the damp, clammy feeling making Jenna want to shake him off and tell him to get lost. Instead, she tolerated his hand on her bare skin and walked out to the dance floor, the chip in the hand Devita wasn't holding. Her mind raced ahead to form a plan to get the disk from her fingers into one of his pockets without being too obvious and alerting him to the fact that he was being bugged.

The band changed music from a swing dance to a slow-moving waltz.

Devita swept her into his arms and whirled her onto the dance floor.

Jenna wasn't expecting a ruthless killer to be so adept at dancing. Careful not to drop the disk, she rested her left hand on his shoulder. This was going to be harder than she'd thought. She had to get her hand down to the pocket at his side to drop the disk into it. Or transfer the disk to her right hand and slip it into his left breast pocket. Since he held her right hand, that wasn't an option. She'd have to manage to slip the disk in when she dropped her hands after the dance.

Completely focused on the mechanics of getting the disk into his pocket, Jenna didn't realize Devita was asking her a question until he repeated it.

"Oh, I'm sorry. I must have been concentrating too hard

on the dance steps." She forced herself to smile up at him. "What is it you were saying?"

"You are an American?"

"Yes, I am."

"In what state do you live?"

"Louisiana." She blinked and acted the young, ditzy woman. "Surely you've heard of New Orleans?"

"*Sí*, senorita. I have heard of the city. You are a very beautiful woman. Not many Mexican senoritas are blessed with such vibrant hair."

She laughed, the sound breathy and tight. "My mother had red hair."

"She must be a very beautiful woman to have a daughter such as you."

Her chest squeezed tight. Her mother had once been the center of her universe. "Sadly, she passed away when I was a young girl." What would she think about her daughter playing the role of covert operative?

Devita slowed. "My apologies for mentioning her."

"Oh, it's all right." Jenna forced a smile. "It was a long time ago."

He swung her away and back into his arms.

If he did it again, Jenna could aim her hand for his waist instead of his shoulder. Then she could slip the disk into his pocket and be done with the subterfuge. She, Carly and Natalie could get up and walk out of the bar without worrying about being attacked or caught in the act of bugging the boss.

Instead of twirling her outward, Devita pulled her close against him. Though the man wore an expensive suit, tailor-made to fit him, and an expensive cologne, his alcohol-laced breath nearly knocked Jenna over. She fought not to gag and remained pressed to his chest swaying to the music, when they should have been waltzing around the room.

"Tell me, pretty lady. What is your name?" he asked, words stirring the loose hairs at the side of her neck, sending cold chills down her spine.

"I'm Jen...nette," she finished quickly, unwilling to use her real name, choosing instead to opt for a form of her name to keep it as close to the truth as possible to cover her faux pas. Damn. She'd almost given the man her real name.

He tipped his head. "Jennette. I am Carmelo." He said it with a flair, his tongue rolling the *r* so easily.

"Nice to meet you." Hell, would he never swing her out and back so that she could drop the disk?

The waltz ended before Devita could swing her out again, and his hands dropped to his sides. With a slight bow, he swept his hand out in the direction of the bar. "It has been a pleasure. I hope to dance with you again."

"Thank you." She let him guide her back to the table, wondering how she would be able to turn or bump into him. Devita walked beside her, his pockets out of reach. There was no way to move her hand closer without making it obvious she was putting her fingers into one.

As they neared the bar, Natalie slipped from the stool. "I'll just make a quick run to the bathroom. Will you watch my seat for me?" she asked. No sooner had she set her feet on the ground than she tripped and banged into Devita, who in turn lurched toward Jenna.

Jenna braced herself for impact, realizing Natalie was setting her up to be crashed into. Her fingers tightened around the disk, afraid she'd drop it if jolted too hard. As Devita stumbled forward, Jenna braced one hand on his chest. The other hand found his pocket and dropped the disk.

One of Devita's men lunged for Natalie, yanking her away from their boss. Another grabbed Devita's arm and helped him upright.

Jenna staggered back, her bottom connecting to the bar stool. She sat down hard. "Oh, my." She pressed her fingertips to her lips. "Are you all right?"

He nodded once, tugging on his suit jacket to straighten it.

Jenna turned to Natalie. "Are you okay?"

"I'm so sorry," she said, reaching out to touch Devita's shoulder. "That was clumsy of me." She glanced at the man who still held her arm in a tight grip. "Thank you for helping me."

Devita's eyes narrowed for a second at Natalie. Then he turned to Jenna, lifted her hand and pressed his lips to the backs of her knuckles. "Until we meet again." He executed an about-face and returned to his table.

His bodyguard released Natalie and followed.

Jenna and Carly both hooked Natalie's arms.

"We'll go with you to the bathroom," Carly said.

"I'm sure I need to powder my nose," Jenna added, ready to make a run for it. "Are you sure you're okay?"

Natalie giggled, a sound so silly coming from an expert marksman. "I must have had too much bourbon." Leaning heavily on Jenna and Carly, she pretended to be a little tipsy and let them help her out of the bar and presumably to the bathroom.

Once they cleared the door to the bar and the men guarding it, Natalie straightened and stepped out, heading for the back of the hotel that led to the boat dock.

Jenna fell in step with Natalie. "Time to go."

Chapter Twelve

Sawyer had been hunkered low in the bougainvillea bush for a good fifteen minutes when he spotted the three truckloads of armed men as they raced toward the hotel.

Devita's guards saw them, too, and rushed forward to meet them before they skidded to a stop in front of the Playa del Sol. Shouts sounded and Devita's men scattered into the darkness, taking up covered positions.

This new development wasn't good. With the women still inside with Devita and what appeared to be a contingent of Devita's rivals on top of them, things were about to go south real fast.

While Devita's men were tied up with approaching trouble, Sawyer saw his chance to fall back and find another way into the building without charging through the front door.

"Rival drug lord rolling up in front of the hotel," Sawyer said into his headset.

"Thought something was funny. The guards at the corners just ran inside an employee entrance," Duff reported.

The sound of gunfire erupted in front of the hotel.

"Can we get inside and find the women?" Sawyer asked.

"We can go in the way the guards did," Duff said.

"Duff and I are going in. Montana, we need you to secure the boat."

"On it," Montana replied.

"Quent?" Sawyer paused.

"Here," Quentin responded. "What's going on?"

"Be ready to bug out ASAP. Devita's rivals decided now would be a good time for gang warfare," Sawyer said. "Duff and I are going in for the ladies." He didn't wait for Quentin's response. Instead, he grabbed the door handle for the back entrance and tugged.

"Needs a key card," Duff noted.

"No, it needs to open." Sawyer pulled the gun from the waistband of his trousers, aimed at the lock and squeezed the trigger.

A single shot blew open the lock, and Sawyer yanked the door open. The corridor was empty. Carrying his nine-millimeter in front of him, his hand on the trigger, Sawyer ran toward the interior of the building, praying Jenna, Carly and Natalie were already on their way out.

Sprinting down the hallway, he slowed as he neared a junction. One of Devita's men barreled around the corner, glancing behind him as he ran.

Sawyer swung his arm, handgun and all, catching the guy in the throat with the barrel of the pistol, crushing his Adam's apple. The man dropped his gun and clutched at his throat, gasping for air.

Sawyer grabbed his arm, shoved him into a one of the conference rooms and dispatched him with a clean sweep of his knife, all in a matter of seconds.

Back in the corridor, he ran toward the end of the hotel where the bar was located, fear for the safety of the women foremost in his mind. The closer he came, the louder the shouts and screams from men and women desperate to get out of the way of the warring factions.

Once again, he came to a junction and slowed. A scream from around the corner made him pick up the pace. As he neared the corner, more sounds of gunfire made his blood run cold. Was he too late to get Jenna out?

"WHICH WAY?" CARLY ASKED.

"I think the bathroom is this way," Natalie said loudly enough the guards behind them could hear.

They headed across the lobby, toward the rear of the hotel.

Before they reached the back doors leading to the board-walk and their boat, the glass doors of the front entrance exploded, shards spraying inward, the sound of gunfire echoing off the high ceilings of the entryway.

"Run!" Natalie yelled and took off for the rear exit.

Jenna lifted her skirt and raced after her.

Men burst through the doors they were aiming for, wielding submachine guns, firing at Devita's men positioned in front of the bar.

Becca Smith appeared in front of Jenna and shouted, "This way!" She grabbed Jenna, Natalie and Carly and shoved them down a hallway, out of the melee of shouting men, screaming women and gunfire.

They ran to the end of the hallway, where another corridor intersected with it.

Carly looked in one direction. "Which way?"

Jenna checked out the other end of the corridor. "There. *Salida*. That means exit." She grabbed Carly's arm and dragged her toward the door. Natalie brought up the rear.

Jenna reached the door first and slammed her body into the lever to open it. The door swung out, and a man dressed all in black brandished a machine gun in their faces and shouted at them in Spanish.

Jenna threw herself to the floor and rolled to the side.

Natalie did the same.

Carly stood frozen.

Becca charged at the frightened woman, hitting her in the backs of the knees, sending her slamming to the hard tiled floor. Then Becca rolled behind a huge potted tree.

The man with the gun shifted his aim downward. Just as he pulled the trigger, he jerked backward, the bullets slamming into the ceiling, nothing but a gurgle coming from his slit throat.

The man fell to the side, and Sawyer waved to the women. "Let's go!"

Jenna, Carly and Natalie scrambled to their feet, kicked off their shoes and ran out the back door of the hotel, following Sawyer to the beach.

The popping sound of gunfire filled the air.

Jenna ran as fast as her bare feet could carry her through the sand, refusing to look behind her, afraid if she slowed, Devita's men would catch up.

Instead of running toward the dock, they ran toward a deserted part of the beach. When Jenna thought her lungs would explode, she spotted the boat Sawyer, Montana and Duff had used to follow them that evening.

Sawyer reached it first and started shoving it toward the water. The tide had gone out, leaving the boat stranded in the wet sand.

Natalie grabbed the side of the boat and helped shove it toward the water.

Carly and Jenna joined Natalie and Sawyer, pushing and shoving the boat toward the sea. It was too heavy and, with the tide so far out, they'd never get it into the water.

About the time Jenna had given up hope, Montana and Duff arrived and threw themselves into pushing the boat out into the surf. A wave rolled in and lifted the hull, giving them just enough help that they could get it out into water deep enough to float.

"Get in!" Sawyer grabbed Jenna and swung her over the side, depositing her in the boat. "Start the motor."

She landed on the floor of the boat, the wind momentarily knocked from her lungs.

Carly flew over the side and landed next to her, upside down, her feet in the air.

Jenna scrambled to her feet, dived for the driver's seat, fumbled for the key and twisted. The motor chugged to life.

Another wave lifted the boat. Duff slipped over the side and landed in the boat, grabbed Natalie's hand and dragged himself aboard. Sawyer and Montana hauled themselves over the side and into the boat.

"Wait." Jenna scanned the beach. "Where's Becca?"

"Who?" Sawyer asked.

"Becca. She helped us get out of the hotel."

"We can't wait," Sawyer said. "Go!"

A barrage of gunfire settled it for Jenna, and she shoved the throttle to the rear. The small boat backed away from the beach. "What about Quentin?"

"He should be out to sea by now. Just go," Sawyer called out. He stepped up behind her, bent over and rested his hand on hers over the steering wheel. Together, they spun the wheel around and shoved the throttle forward, taking the little boat far enough away from Playa del Sol to avoid stray bullets.

Or so they hoped.

"We've got a tail!" Natalie shouted.

They rose and fell in the waves as they pushed past the shore and out into the open water.

Bullets flew past them.

"They'll catch us at this rate," Duff said. "We have more people on board than they do. It's slowing us down."

"Would it help if I jumped?" Carly asked.

"No!" responded everyone on board.

The boat behind them slowly closed the distance between them. Starlight revealed the men aboard wielded automatic weapons.

"Everyone down!" Sawyer yelled, shoving Jenna to the floor. He hunkered low, but high enough to see over the dash to the ocean ahead. He twisted the steering wheel right, then left, zigzagging through the water. Bullets peppered the hull. Some slammed into the windshield, shattering the glass.

Sawyer tossed his gun to Jenna. "Know how to use one of these?" he asked.

She fumbled but caught it. "Not really."

"Then drive this boat."

She slipped in front of Sawyer and took the helm, her hand resting on the throttle, her insides quaking.

"They're coming in range," Sawyer shouted. "On my mark, I want you to shift the throttle all the way back to Neutral." He waited until the trailing boat was almost upon them. "Now!"

Jenna pulled the throttle back, bringing the boat to an abrupt stop in the water.

The craft behind them swerved, barely missing them. All the men aboard the other boat teetered, grabbing for purchase as the boat tipped precariously.

Sawyer, Montana and Natalie all aimed their weapons and fired at the other boat. Duff aimed for the motor and fired all of his bullets into the engine. Smoke billowed from the casing and rose into the night sky, fogging the stars.

Sawyer shifted into Forward and spun the little boat away, putting as much distance between them and Devita's men as possible.

Soon he noticed another boat's lights blinking in the night. "Get ready in case it's Devita," he warned the others.

"I'm out of ammo," Duff said.

"Me, too," Natalie added.

Montana released his magazine and reported, "Five rounds. We better make them count."

"I think I have ten left," Sawyer said, aiming his weapon at the other boat.

"Hey, don't shoot!" Quentin's voice sounded in Sawyer's ear through the headset. "We just barely got out with my skin still intact."

Sawyer drew in a deep breath and let it out. He turned to Jenna. "Want me to take the helm?"

"Yes!" Jenna gladly let Sawyer slide in front of her and she eased out but stood beside him, rocking with the waves, staring at the dark ink of the ocean before them. "Is your life always this insane?"

Sawyer slipped an arm around her waist and pulled her against him. "Sometimes even more so. Stick around. You're likely to find out just how crazy we are, too."

JENNA WAS HAPPY to get back to the marina and the luxurious yacht. Quentin and Montana had gone ahead and were waiting when the rest of the team arrived.

"What the hell happened back there?" Quentin asked.

Duff snorted and dropped onto one of the white leather sofas. "We had a little altercation with some of Devita's men. At least, I think they were Devita's. When their rivals showed up, it was difficult to tell who belonged to which cartel."

"I'm glad we all made it out safely." Natalie eased into Duff's lap and wrapped her arms around his neck.

Jenna envied Duff and Natalie's ease with each other. She was amazed they'd known each other for only about a week. The woman appeared unruffled by all that had happened, while Jenna's head was still spinning from being shot at and nearly killed. She glanced down at her beautiful dress, a little wrinkled and damp from their dash through the hotel and pushing the boat out into the water. She hoped the salt water didn't stain the fabric.

"The question is, did you tag Devita with the tracking device?"

Natalie grinned and stared across the room at Jenna. "Jenna caught his eye. Apparently Devita likes redheads."

Jenna's cheeks heated. "The man definitely likes red hair. And yes, I managed to drop the chip into his pocket thanks to some...uh—" her lips twitched "—fancy footwork by Natalie."

Natalie laughed. "She means I fake-tripped, slamming into Devita, shoving him up against Jenna so she could get her hand into his pocket and drop the bug."

Carly smiled. "They were amazing. And Jenna was as cool as a professional spy, dancing with the man. You should have seen her."

Sawyer stepped up behind Jenna and whispered, "I'd rather have been dancing with you." He rested his hands on her shoulders. "I never should have let you go tonight. It was far too dangerous."

She gave him a sideways glance. "And we did just fine."

"Damn right, you did." Lance sat at his laptop. "Devita is on the move. Ideally he's headed back to his compound. I'd like to get as much information as I can on the layout before you attempt an infiltration into the lion's den. I think I can tap into one of the CIA's satellites. It should be going over this area sometime in the next couple of hours."

"Let us know as soon as you get a clear image. The sooner we get to Devita, the sooner we resolve this nightmare," Sawyer said.

"In the meantime," Duff said, "we should conserve our

energy. We might be infiltrating Devita's compound to-night or tomorrow. Either way, we need sleep."

Natalie slipped off his lap and stood. "I think it's a safe bet to assume it might not be smart for us to return to the resort at this time."

"Even if it was safe, it's getting pretty late." Duff stared around at the people in the room. "This yacht can sleep all of us. I suggest you stake a claim on a room and rest up."

"I'll take the first watch tonight," Montana offered. "Lance might need help going through the images."

"Wake me in four hours," Quentin said. "I'll take the next watch."

"All of my things are back at the hotel," Jenna said. "I could call a cab."

"No, you're not exactly safe," Sawyer said. "We still don't know who the assassin is, but he knows who you are. You can't go back in the middle of the night."

"Each stateroom is equipped with a bathrobe, spare pajamas and toiletries," Quentin said. "And if you don't have everything you need in your room, the steward's cabin has a supply cabinet with everything from shampoo to spare razors."

Jenna shrugged. "Then I guess I'll call it a night." She headed down the stairs to the lower deck.

Footsteps made her turn to see who had followed her down.

Her heart skipped several beats when she realized Sawyer was right behind her.

"You can choose whichever room you like."

She pushed a door open to a stateroom with a full-size bed, the bright white sheets a stark contrast to the wood features stained a deep, rich mahogany. "Which one will you be in?" Jenna held her breath, wondering if he'd think she was coming on to him and half hoping he would. After all that had happened that day and evening, she didn't want to be alone. She wanted Sawyer beside her.

Hands descended on her shoulders and turned her around. "I'll be in the room you choose."

Her heart thumping hard against her ribs, Jenna cocked her brows and tilted her chin. "Is that so?"

Sawyer bent to brush his lips across hers. "Yes. I want to be with you."

Who was she kidding? She wanted to be with him as badly as he wanted to be with her. Jenna reached behind her and shoved the door closed. "This room will do." Rising up on her toes, she pressed her lips to his, wrapped her arms around his neck and pulled him close. She opened her mouth to him, meeting his tongue with hers, thirstily drinking in the essence of the man.

For a long moment, they shared a kiss that rocked Jenna's soul. The need to be closer drove her to drag his T-shirt over his head.

He pushed the straps of her dress over her shoulders and the garment dropped to her waist, exposing her bare breasts.

Jenna let her head drop back, allowing Sawyer to trail kisses down the long line of her throat, and lower, to capture a beaded nipple between his teeth.

A moan rose up her throat and escaped on a gasp as he sucked her breast into his mouth, pulling hard. Then he tongued the nipple, flicking the tip until a tug lower in her belly made her yearn for so much more.

Jenna reached behind her and loosened the zipper on the dress. The green fabric slipped past her hips and pooled at her bare feet. Where her rhinestone stilettoes were, she didn't know, nor did she care. She was naked, standing in front of a man who'd been a complete stranger only days before. Yet she'd never felt closer or more compelled to give herself to a man than she wanted to give herself to Sawyer. She backed away from him until her thighs bumped into the bed. "Make love to me," she whispered.

"No regrets in the morning?"

"The only regret I have now is that I didn't meet you sooner." As he closed the distance between them, her pulse sped and her breathing became more difficult, desire washing over her in a tidal wave of need.

Sawyer caught her face between his hands. "I'm no good at relationships."

Her chest tightened. She wanted more, but she'd take any time she could get from him. "I'm only asking for the night." Jenna ran her hands down his chest to the button on his jeans and flicked it open.

Sawyer kissed her, his hands sliding down her back to cup her bottom. He lifted her, settling her on the edge of the bed, nudging her knees apart with his thigh.

Gently Jenna tugged at his zipper, dragging it down. His shaft sprang free into her hand, and she caressed him, reveling in the smooth hardness.

"Keep that up and I won't be able to control myself."

"Who said I wanted you to?" Her lips curved and she tipped her head back, thrusting her chest forward. "Maybe I want you to lose control."

Sawyer dragged in a deep breath. He stepped back enough to kick off his shoes and shove his jeans down his legs. Stepping out of the denim, he stood in front of her, naked, his body a testament to his dedication to being physically fit, capable of performing the hardest job on the planet.

Jenna scooted back on the bed, making room for the big SEAL.

Sawyer crawled up between her legs and leaned over her. "I don't suppose you thought about protection?"

She shook her head, a chuckle rising up her throat. "No, I really wasn't thinking much at all."

"This place is pretty well equipped. You don't suppose…" Sawyer leaned over her to reach into the nightstand anchored to the floor.

While Sawyer rummaged in the drawer, Jenna ran her hands over the hard planes of his body, loving how solid he was in every way.

"Ha!" He held up an accordion of foil packets and grinned. "I don't know who owns this boat, but he's obviously prepared for everything."

"Let me." Jenna took the accordion, ripped one of the packets free and tore it open.

Sawyer leaned back, giving her access to that hard, thick shaft.

Jenna shivered in anticipation as she rolled the condom over him. Then she lay back on the sheets and guided him to her entrance.

With the tip of his shaft edging into her warm, wet channel, Sawyer paused and kissed the tip of her nose. "What? No foreplay?"

"It's overrated when your body is already on fire." She grabbed his hips and brought him home.

He slid inside her, his thickness filling her, stretching her. Jenna dragged in a deep breath and let it out slowly.

Sawyer leaned close, his lips touching her earlobe. "Are you all right?"

"Yes!" she cried. Then she eased him out and back in. "More than all right."

He laughed. "Just checking." He settled into a steady rhythm, driving in and out, increasing in speed and intensity.

Jenna brought her knees up and dug her heels into the mattress, raising her hips to meet his every thrust.

He rode her hard, and she wanted it even harder as she catapulted over the edge, the explosion of sensations rocketing through her, sending electrical shocks throughout her body.

Sawyer thrust once more, burying himself deep inside, his body rigid, his face tight. He stayed frozen for a long moment, his breath caught and held. Then he released the breath and dropped down on Jenna, rolling her with him to his side.

"You are amazing," he said, kissing her cheek, her eyes and finally her lips.

"I was going to say the same thing." Jenna snuggled into his body, loving that they retained their intimate connection. Her eyelids drifted closed and she yawned. "I could get used to this."

Sawyer's arms tightened.

As Jenna slipped into a deep sleep, she thought she heard Sawyer whisper, "So could I."

Chapter Thirteen

A light tap on the door woke Sawyer. He glanced at the clock on the nightstand. Two in the morning. He'd been asleep for less than two hours, resting comfortably with Jenna in his arms.

Another tap brought him fully alert. He slipped out of the bed, careful not to wake the beauty lying beside him.

He padded naked to the door and opened it.

Duff stood there dressed all in black, his face camouflaged black, as well. "We have intel. The sooner we move on it, the better."

"I'm ready."

Duff grinned, his teeth bright white in his blackened face. "You might want to put some clothes on."

Sawyer closed the door, slipped into his black jeans and grabbed his shoes and shirt. Before he left, he bent and brushed his lips across Jenna's, wishing he could stay and wake with her in his arms.

In the lounge, he shoved his feet into his shoes. "What do you have?" he asked as he dragged his dark T-shirt over his head.

Lance brought up an image on a large monitor housed in a cabinet. "I was able to track Devita to this location." He pointed to a position on the map. "It appears to be a remote, deserted island off the northern tip of the Yucatán

Peninsula. I tapped into the CIA's satellite images. Seems they've been keeping an eye on our man Devita and have this compound tagged. He's got others, but this is the one he went to tonight." Lance touched the mouse, and a satellite image replaced the map. In the image, a sprawling structure could be seen with a wall around the outside and several buildings within.

"From what I could deduce from the pictures and the supporting documentation, the largest structure is Devita's home. If you want to get to him, you have to breach the wall and enter through here—" with the cursor, he pointed to the front "—or here." Lance moved the cursor to the rear of the building. "The windows are too high on the exterior walls. There is a courtyard in the center, but you'd have to get inside the structure to access it, so it will be of no use to you."

Quentin and Montana climbed up the stairs from the lower level, carrying backpacks and submachine guns.

Natalie followed with a couple of helmets and handguns.

"I've got the fireworks." Montana held up a handful of plastic explosives.

"I have the detonators in my backpack," Quentin said. He snagged the packages from Montana. "I'll take those."

Montana tossed a submachine gun at Sawyer and a vest equipped with a body-armor plate. "I can't get over the number of MP5SDs this yacht is equipped with."

"Good. We might need the sound suppression if we want to get to Devita without alerting his entire army." Sawyer slipped the vest over his shoulders and buckled the front. Attached to the vest were several thirty-round magazines for the MP5SD submachine gun.

Natalie had lined the coffee table with the helmets equipped with night-vision goggles. She'd also brought along several P226 handguns. "You might need something a little more personal."

"Are you coming along?" Sawyer asked Natalie.

She shook her head. "I'm staying to help Lance keep the ladies out of trouble."

Sawyer nodded. "Thanks."

"I'd rather go with you, but I don't want to slow you down. You SEALs are better trained at this kind of operation than I am."

Quentin selected one of the handguns. "I want to meet the guy who owns this yacht. He's got great taste in equipment."

"How are we getting to Devita's compound?" Sawyer asked.

"The best way would be to go in by helicopter, but that's one piece of equipment this yacht didn't come equipped with," Montana said.

Duff pointed to the map. "We're going as far as we can up a river by boat. From there, we'll go on foot. It's about a mile from the river to the compound. Shouldn't take more than thirty minutes."

"If the jungle isn't too thick," Quentin added. "And we don't run into any guards along the way."

"When do we leave?" Sawyer asked.

Duff slipped into his vest, slid a P226 into the holster at his hip and grabbed one of the helmets. "Now."

They climbed down from the yacht and loaded into the boat they'd taken to Playa del Sol.

"Would be nice if we had one of our SEAL team's riverboats," Quentin groused.

"We're lucky to have this one," Duff said.

"Okay." Quentin waved at Duff. "I get it. Be grateful for what we have."

Natalie stood on the dock, handing over weapons. "Don't do anything stupid."

Duff was last to get in. He paused as he stood beside Natalie. "I'll be back."

"I'm counting on it. We still have another week of vacation to kill before going back to our real lives. I'd like to spend it with you." She cupped his blackened face. "You look good in makeup." She kissed him, and Duff crushed her to his chest for a brief moment. Then he climbed aboard.

Sawyer's insides tightened. What he wouldn't give to have one last kiss, one last hug from Jenna before he left for a mission he wasn't certain he'd come out of alive. It was better to let her sleep through their departure than to make promises he wasn't sure he could keep. All the more reason not to get too involved with a woman.

He couldn't get over Duff being as optimistic as he was with Natalie. But then, she knew better than anyone the risks of the job. She was a secret agent and ran covert operations that could lead to her own early demise.

Jenna was an accountant. Until she'd run into him, she hadn't known the dangers involved in the life of a navy SEAL.

Quentin untied the line and pushed the small boat out into the channel leaving the Puerto Cancún marina.

They'd follow the coastline north and then cut across the open water, swinging wide of the island. The plan was to land on the northwest side and then go the rest of the way on foot. If they were lucky, they'd get in, obtain the information they wanted from Devita and leave before his men had any idea they'd been attacked.

Duff manned the helm, steering the small craft past the city of Cancún, lit up by street, garden and security lights on the corners of resort hotels and scattered over the campuses. The idea was to give the tourists a sense of safety, no matter how thinly veiled. Despite the beauty of the tall buildings and the highly lit yards and gardens, there was still something decidedly unsettling about the beach resort.

"Been thinking," Quentin said from his seat behind Sawyer.

"That's a dangerous pastime for you, Quent."

Quentin grinned good-naturedly. "I know. But a man does that when he starts to get older."

"What were you on your last birthday? Twenty-nine?" Montana asked.

"Thirty," Quentin responded.

Duff shot a glance in Quentin's direction. "With all that thinking, what conclusions have you come to?"

"It might be time to do something else besides be a navy frogman."

"What?" Sawyer feigned surprise. Quentin had made similar comments over the past year. "I thought you liked your brothers in arms."

Quentin raised a hand as if he was a courtroom witness swearing to tell the truth. "Oh, I do. I'd take a bullet for any one of you."

Duff rubbed his shoulder. "You could have done that earlier and I wouldn't be aching now."

"That's just it." Quentin stared out at the ocean, illuminated by starlight. "Our bodies will eventually be too battered to do this job properly. We have to make way for the younger SEALs to make their mark."

Montana puffed up his chest. "I don't know about you, but this body is in prime shape."

"Until you take a bullet or shrapnel once too often. Traumatic brain injury, torn ligaments, hearing loss. You name it. It could happen to you in training or in the field.

What then? Have you made any plans for your transition out of the military, into civilian life?"

Duff scratched his chin. "I could always go to work for SOS with Natalie."

Sawyer frowned at his friend. "Have you really been thinking about giving up the SEALs?"

Duff shrugged. "It's crossed my mind lately."

"Anything to do with one sexy, kick-ass blonde?" Quentin asked.

With a nod, Duff answered, "Some. It's hard to have a relationship when the parts of the whole aren't in the same state, much less the same country."

"You barely know Natalie," Montana observed.

Duff's lips curled. "I know enough. And I'd like to get to know her even better."

An image flashed through Sawyer's mind of Jenna sleeping peacefully back in the stateroom aboard the yacht. He'd like to get to know her better, too, but part of him held back, wondering why he should bother. She was an accountant. That kept her in one place. He was a SEAL who could be called to duty at a moment's notice. A relationship between them was doomed to fail.

Hadn't his father taught him that? His mother divorced his father because she didn't like being alone more than they were together. As a child, Sawyer saw more of his nanny than he did either of his parents. What little time his father was home, he spent glued to his desk, shuffling papers or talking to someone on the phone. "Relationships are hard when you're never together."

"My point exactly." Duff tipped his head toward the bow. "We're coming up on the island. Gear up. We're going in."

Sawyer plunked his helmet on his head and secured the strap, pushing all other thoughts to the back of his mind.

They had a mission to accomplish, and he couldn't be distracted by something he could never have.

JENNA WOKE TO the sound of a small engine revving beside the little porthole of the stateroom. She sat up with a start and looked to the empty pillow next to her.

The engine revved again and settled into a rumbling hum, slowly fading.

She knelt in the bed and pushed aside the curtain to see a small motorboat pulling away from the yacht with four dark shadows of men hunkered low in the seats.

Sawyer was gone.

Throwing aside the sheet, she climbed out of the bed and rummaged through the drawers, finding a men's extra-large soft blue T-shirt and a pair of men's swim shorts with a drawstring. She slipped into the shorts, pulled the drawstring tight and knotted the T-shirt at her waist to keep it from dragging around her knees. Then she started up the stairs to the lounge area.

Before she reached the top, the yacht's engines fired up, and the vessel shimmied. Jenna stopped halfway up the stairs and held on to the railing. They were moving.

She sprinted to the top and strode into the lounge, where Natalie hovered around the computer monitor. The image displayed was a map of the Yucatán Peninsula with two blinking dots. One was moving across the blue patch of ocean. The other was on a small island off the northern tip of the peninsula.

Jenna pointed to the moving dot. "Is that the guys?"

Natalie nodded. "They should be there in approximately thirty minutes."

"And we're going, too?" she asked.

"We're going part of the way." Natalie stared at the

monitor, her brows puckered. "We won't be involved in the actual event."

"Are we moving?" Carly staggered up the stairs, yawning.

"Yes," Jenna said, staring out the window as they drifted by the lights of Puerto Cancún.

Carly yawned again and stretched. She wore a men's pajama top and nothing else. Dropping her arms to her sides, she stared around the lounge. "Where are the guys?"

"Going after Devita." Jenna returned to the monitor and watched for a while, her stomach knotted, her insides jumpy. "I feel so useless. Isn't there anything we can do to help them?"

Natalie shook her head. "They have to get in and out on their own. They will have the ability to contact us on the two-way radio, but there isn't much we can do from the yacht."

"If they get in a tight spot, could we get close enough to the island to extract them?" Carly asked.

"It would be risky, and they'd have to meet us in the water. The only dock on the island will be heavily guarded. We do, however, have a small dinghy, if we need to go get them." Natalie tapped her fingers on the desk.

"Are they terribly outnumbered?" Jenna questioned, her voice weak, fear for Sawyer making her shiver in the air-conditioned lounge.

"We can only guess." Natalie continued to stare at the blinking dot on the monitor. She appeared as worried as Jenna felt.

"Are you and Duff serious?" Jenna asked. "You don't have to tell me, if you don't want to."

Natalie shot a glance her way and then returned her attention to the monitor. "I just met the man less than a week ago."

Jenna smiled. "Do you believe in love at first sight?"

"Not really. But I believe Duff and I have a connection that neither of us can ignore." She gave Jenna a weak smile. "I don't know where it will go or how long it will last."

"But you're willing to give it a shot?"

Natalie's smile widened. "Yeah. I guess I am. He's an amazingly strong but sensitive man. He's a trained killer, but he's the gentlest soul I've ever encountered. He gets me." She shook her head, staring at the monitor again. "I think I could fall in love with him." She glanced at Jenna, her eyes shining bright, the truth written in the happiness on her face. "If I haven't already."

Jenna's heart tightened. How did someone fall in love in a matter of days, maybe only hours? Was it possible? Did love at first sight exist?

She remembered Sawyer standing behind her on the zip-line platform. His laughing eyes and concern over plummeting to his death on a thin cable had melted her heart from the very first moment her gaze met his. Love at first sight? Maybe not, but admiration and attraction… you bet your life.

Now he was on his way to infiltrate Devita's secret compound. If he didn't come back…

Jenna's heart skipped several beats and raced on to catch up. Having known Sawyer for so short a time, she couldn't believe herself to be in love with the man. But lust and desire had been off the charts and incredible.

For a woman who had thought no man other than Tyler would capture her attention and maybe even her heart, Jenna had been so very wrong. Sawyer was more man than Tyler had ever dreamed of being. Jenna felt a little sorry for her former maid of honor being stuck with the coward.

Nah. They deserved each other for the crappy way

they'd treated her. Jenna gave their relationship three months before they split up.

Tyler might even try to come back to her.

Jenna snorted softly. Never in a million years would she take him back. Not after having Sawyer in her life and in her bed.

Too wound up to go back to sleep and frankly too scared to leave the lounge, Jenna curled up on one of the white leather sofas and waited. When they got closer, she might consider guarding the decks and searching the water for the small motorboat and the man she'd come to admire. A man she could easily fall in love with.

God, she was a fool! From a man who didn't love her to another man who refused to get that involved, she sure knew how to pick them and make her life miserable.

Chapter Fourteen

They'd come ashore unnoticed, sliding the small motorboat up onto the sand near a small outcropping of brush.

Fully equipped with observation equipment, guns and ammo, they could make this mission happen.

Sawyer lay in the brush, eyeing the compound fence through his night-vision goggles. So far he hadn't spotted any green heat signatures indicating warm bodies and guards.

"If we're going, we'd better do it now. There are only a couple more hours until morning. I don't want to be here when the sun comes up," Duff said into his headset.

"Agreed," Sawyer responded. "Let's do this." He took off running.

Duff did, as well. When they reached the eight-foot wall, Duff cupped his hand. Sawyer stepped into it and launched himself over the top.

He landed in the soft, sandy soil on the other side and flattened himself to the earth, staring through his goggles, looking for any sign of movement or heat. So far nothing.

"Clear," he whispered into his headset to the others.

A second later, Duff flew over the top of the wall and landed beside Sawyer.

Montana was next, but he stopped at the top of the wall

and reached back to haul Quentin over. They landed on the ground making no sound at all.

The main building was fifty feet to the south. Nothing moved in the dead of the night except the guards standing watch at the entrance to the house and on the corners of the buildings.

The team split. Montana took the north corner while Quentin, Sawyer and Duff headed for the south corner and the rear entrance.

Sawyer sprinted ahead and caught the corner guard unaware, dispatching him with his knife. The man went down.

Duff and Quentin dragged him into the brush.

Sawyer found a back entrance locked, as he'd expected. He pulled his P226 handgun, fixed a silencer on it and blew a hole through the lock. The door swung open into a laundry room. None of the machines were running and the lights were out, but a light shone through from under the door leading into the house.

Sawyer shifted his night-vision goggles up on his helmet and eased the door open into a hallway with doors leading off each side.

Montana and Duff entered the laundry room behind him.

"Quent?" Sawyer whispered into his microphone.

"Checking all corners and setting charges." The explosives would help create a diversion should they need it.

Sawyer moved down the hallway to a door half-open. The lingering scent of food drifted through. Easing the door fully open, he noted the kitchen with a single light burning over the sink. It was empty and shut down for the night.

Closing the door, Sawyer continued down the hallway and came into a large dining room with a long formal table and a dozen chairs situated around the solid wood surface. The dining room opened into a foyer with a sweeping staircase leading to the upper level of the mansion.

A guard leaned against the wall to the right of the front entrance, his chin touching his chest, his eyes closed.

Sawyer crept up to the man and took him out with a quick slash across his throat. Easing him to the floor, Sawyer nodded to Montana and Duff. They split up, ducking through every door on the lower level, checking for any other guards or people who might be around and cause them trouble. Sawyer started up the stairs, crouching low and hugging the railing. As he reached the top, he noted another guard sitting on the floor in front of a broad wooden doorway. His head was resting against the door frame and his weapon lay across his lap. The man was sound asleep.

As Sawyer neared him, he jerked in his sleep, his head banging against the wooden door. He blinked and stared up at Sawyer. His eyes widened and his mouth opened. Before he could shout, Sawyer dispatched him and dragged him away from the door. This had to be Devita's room.

Montana and Duff arrived on the landing as Sawyer turned the knob.

"Uh, we might have a problem here," Quentin said into Sawyer's headset.

Sawyer paused before pushing the door in.

"Clarify," Montana whispered, farther back from the door than Sawyer.

"I hear an engine overhead," Quentin said. "I think it's a drone."

Sawyer's pulse leaped. What the hell was a drone doing flying over Devita's place?

Sawyer eased the door open and rushed into the room.

A huge mahogany bed with a canopy along the top took up the majority of one wall. Sawyer had crossed the room before the man in the bed knew what was happening. He grabbed Devita and yanked him out of the bed, pressing a knife to his throat.

The woman who'd been asleep beside him squealed and gathered the sheet up over her naked body. She rattled off words in Spanish, sobbing at the same time.

"Tell me who you hired to kidnap or kill Senator Houston's son and I'll let you live."

"No comprendo," he said, his head tipped back to avoid the blade.

"He does not speak *Inglés*," said the sobbing woman. She spoke to Devita in Spanish.

Devita gave a tight shake of his head and responded.

The woman said, "He does not know what you are talking about."

"Then why did he have Ramirez deliver a case with weapons and instructions to the hotel if he wasn't the one who hired the assassin?"

Again, the woman translated what Sawyer said. When Devita spoke, he sneered.

The woman bit her lip and hesitated.

Devita barked an order at her and she jumped.

"He was paid a lot of American dollars to deliver the case unopened. Had he known a senator's son was in Cancún, he would have kidnapped him himself and demanded money for his release."

Sawyer's gut knotted and anger ripped through him. This effort to discover his tormentor could not be a failure. "Who was supposed to get the case?"

Before Devita could respond, an explosion shook the mansion. Walls cracked and debris shook loose from the ceiling.

"Get out now!" Quentin shouted into the headset. "That drone I told you about just launched a rocket."

Montana zip-tied Devita's wrists and ankles. "What about the woman?"

"Bind her. Make it quick."

The woman struggled, but was no match for Montana. He had her zip-tied in seconds.

Sawyer jerked his head toward the door. "Go!"

Duff and Montana raced for the bedroom door. Sawyer brought up the rear. Weapons at the ready, the SEALs ran down the staircase and made it all the way through the dining room when the front door burst open and Devita's men crowded through, heading for the staircase.

Sawyer's team had rounded the corner and was headed down the long hallway when another explosion ripped through the center of the house. They were thrown to the floor, but the walls held. Sawyer scrambled to his feet, helped Montana and Duff up and hustled them out the back door, debris and a dust following them through.

They rounded the side of the mansion, headed for the point where they'd breached the wall. Quentin waited in the shadows with his hand cupped.

Montana went over the wall first, followed by Duff. Sawyer went next, stopping on top to grab Quentin's hand and haul him up.

Quentin dropped to the ground on the other side. As Sawyer started to slide off the top, something slammed into his shoulder.

He toppled to the ground, hitting hard.

Duff and Montana grabbed his arms and helped him to his feet.

"You're bleeding," Duff said. He pulled his hand away. It was covered in blood.

"Flesh wound," Sawyer said through gritted teeth. "Get out of here!"

As they ran for the beach where they'd left the small

boat, Montana spoke into the two-way radio. "Took hits from a drone. Sawyer wounded. Getting out. Need backup."

JENNA HEARD THE crackle of the radio and ran across the lounge to Natalie, who held one of the other two-way radios.

"Roger," Lance's disembodied voice responded from his position up top at the helm of the yacht. "Coming in to rendezvous. Got you on the tracker."

Natalie shoved the two-way radio at Jenna. "Hold this. If the drone is targeting the guys, we need to be ready."

She ran for the stairs to the deck below. In less than two minutes, she was back carrying a gun and a box of shells.

"Either of you ever fire a shotgun?" she asked.

Carly nodded. "I have on my uncle's farm."

"It's been a long time, but I used to go duck hunting with my dad in the bayous of Mississippi," Jenna said.

"You're hired. Load up and get out on deck." Natalie handed the weapon and the box of ammunition to Jenna. She glanced at Carly. "Come with me."

The two women ran down the stairs.

Jenna fumbled with the shotgun, trying to remember everything her father taught her about handling one. After several seconds studying the gun, she managed to load the shells. Then she ran out on deck.

"They're a half of a mile off the bow," Lance called out from the helm. "Watch the sky for a drone, and for God's sake, don't shoot our guys."

Her heart pounding, Jenna ran to the front of the yacht, the shotgun heavy in her hands. But, damn it, she'd do whatever it took to protect the men escaping Devita's island. She hooked the two-way radio to the waistband of her shorts and lifted the shotgun to her shoulder, like her father had taught her, settling it into the soft pocket of her shoulder.

A few minutes later, Carly and Natalie joined her, each carrying a weapon. Carly held another shotgun. Natalie carried a rifle with an infrared scope and a submachine gun.

The yacht powered through the water, racing to meet the men.

"We should see them in the next five minutes," Lance called out. "Watch for them."

The stars shone down on the water, the sun a couple of hours from rising. Jenna strained to see any movement on the water other than the gentle swells.

"There!" Lance shouted from above. "Eleven o'clock, two hundred yards. Closing fast."

Jenna scanned the rippling waves. A boat appeared out of the darkness, speeding toward them. Her heart leaped for joy.

"Watch for the drone," Natalie ordered.

Jenna shifted her focus to the sky over the boat carrying Sawyer and his teammates. She couldn't see anything flying over them.

"There's another boat coming in fast!" Lance yelled. "Be ready to provide cover."

The boat carrying the SEALs was within a football field of the yacht when another boat came at them from the starboard side, nearly crashing into them. Shots were fired from the driver of the attacking boat.

Jenna aimed her shotgun at the attacking boat. It was still too far out for her to hit anything. She raised the gun, aimed at the attacker and fired.

At the same time, the attacking boat turned sharply. The hull of the boat rose out of the water and blocked the bullet. The driver swung around behind the SEALs' boat, taking fire from the SEALs but coming at them relentlessly. Gunning the throttle, the attacker raised the bow of the boat high, running fast at the SEAL team's boat, again the hull of the boat between the driver and the bullets being fired at him.

"Damn!" Lance called out. "There's another boat."

Sawyer's boat turned sharply away from the yacht.

"What are they doing?" Jenna asked.

"Taking the firefight away from us," Natalie said through tight lips.

"But we can help." Jenna watched as the boat carrying Sawyer spun away and the men on board fired on the attacking boat.

"They don't see the other boat," Carly said.

"What's he doing?" Jenna watched as the third boat, a long, sleek cigarette jet boat, raced for the attacking boat, throttle wide-open. The driver of the boat that had been attacking the SEALs apparently hadn't noticed the new boat headed straight for him until too late.

Jenna bit her lip and flinched as the cigarette boat crashed into the attacking boat. The two vessels exploded, sending a fireball of flame into the sky. "Oh, my God, the driver did that on purpose."

The SEAL team circled back to the wreckage.

Lance slowed the yacht and edged toward them, finally bringing the bigger boat to a stop.

Jenna ran to the edge of the yacht and leaned over the side, staring down into the water. She counted the men in the SEALs' boat. Four. "Thank God," she whispered.

"Help!" A shout rose up from the water near the wrecked speedboats.

Lance maneuvered the yacht around the smoldering wreck and stopped the vessel. A figure in a bulky life jacket raised a hand in the air. "Help!"

Jenna was surprised. The voice was feminine. She hurried to grab the life preserver and line and tossed it over the side to the woman below.

The woman swam toward the life preserver and hooked her arm through it.

Holding on to the line, Jenna walked to the back of the yacht, pulling the woman along the side. Carly helped haul her toward the ladder. Once she reached the ladder, the woman climbed aboard.

Jenna gasped. In the exterior deck lights, she recognized the woman. "Becca?"

"Hey, Jenna. Thanks for helping me out." Becca unbuckled the life jacket and let it drop to the deck. A dark wetsuit encased her trim body, accentuating her curves. She pushed her hair out of her face and looked back at the water below. "Did you find the driver of the other boat?"

"There!" Lance pointed to a body floating among the splintered debris. He leaned from the door of the helm enclosure and shouted down to the SEALs. "Can you get to him?"

"We'll do what we can. We're taking on water pretty fast, and Sawyer's leaking blood like a sieve," Quentin called out.

Jenna's breath caught and she leaned over the side of the rail, trying to see for herself. Carly rushed up beside her and shone a flashlight down on the boat below.

"I'm fine," Sawyer said. "Just a flesh wound."

Duff eased the boat into the shards of fiberglass. The SEALs grabbed the man out of the water and hauled him onto the boat.

The next second, all hell broke loose, and the men were shouting. Steel glinted in the flashlight's beam.

"He's got a knife!" Montana yelled too late to stop the man they'd hauled aboard from sinking it into Sawyer.

Jenna screamed and was halfway over the rail when Carly dragged her back onto the deck.

Montana, Quentin and Duff tackled the man and dragged him away from Sawyer.

Sawyer clutched the knife protruding from his belly. "Okay, this might not be a flesh wound," he said. When he moved to pull the knife from his gut, three SEALs shouted at once, "Don't move it!"

Jenna couldn't breathe, her heart lodged in her throat and tears rolled down her cheeks. She stood frozen to the deck, staring down at the man who'd touched her like no other. And he might at that moment be dying.

Duff left the attacker to Montana and Quentin and knelt at Sawyer's side.

Lance dropped down from the helm. "Let's get the sling over the side and haul him onto the deck." Natalie and Becca sprang into action, swinging a miniature boom around to the side of the yacht and dropping the cable equipped with a sling to the boat below.

"I'll get the first-aid kit." Carly ran into the lounge and returned a few seconds later with the kit they'd used to patch Duff's injury not so long ago.

Duff helped Sawyer into the sling and gave a thumbs-up.

Lance flipped a switch and the cable tightened, slowly raising Sawyer into the air. When he was high enough, they swung the arm of the boom over the deck and eased Sawyer down onto the surface.

Jenna dropped to her knees beside him and stared in horror at the knife buried in his belly. For a moment, panic threatened to overwhelm her. "When I said I didn't want to live a boring life, I didn't mean for you to go to all the trouble of making it exciting, just for me." She forced a laugh that sounded more like a sob.

Carly moved in, shoving Jenna aside. "We need to sta-bilize the knife until we can get him to a hospital."

Natalie brought towels and the first-aid kit.

Jenna gave Carly room to work, but stayed at Saw-yer's side.

Sawyer reached up with a bloody hand and brushed his knuckle across her cheek. "This ain't nothing, sweetheart."

She snorted. "Yeah, I bet all the SEALs say that." She'd seen the movies. They didn't end well.

"I'll be okay." He tipped his head to the side. "I'm more worried about getting blood on the deck from the wound in my shoulder."

Pushing aside the panic, Jenna held out her hand. "Got a pair of scissors in that kit, Carly?"

Carly opened the first-aid kit and handed Jenna a pair of scissors. "We need to focus on stopping the bleeding."

Jenna cut away the fabric of his T-shirt and pushed it aside to stare down at the ripped corner of Sawyer's shoul-der. The coppery scent of blood filled the air. Forcing back her gag reflex, she went to work, focusing on stopping the flow of blood from Sawyer's shoulder by applying a pres-sure bandage to the front and one to the back where a bul-let had entered. She was careful not to interfere with what Carly was doing to stabilize the protruding knife.

As Jenna worked over Sawyer, the rest of Sawyer's team climbed aboard the yacht, dragging with them the man who'd stabbed Sawyer.

Chapter Fifteen

Jenna placed her body between Sawyer and the man who'd tried to kill him, even though the attacker didn't look as if he had anything left in him for a repeat performance. He bled from several wounds, his face pale and his lips a deepening shade of bluish-purple. Montana and Quentin laid him on the deck, far enough away from Sawyer that the man couldn't do him any harm.

"Who are you?" Duff asked the man.

"What's it matter?" the man responded, his voice raspy. He coughed weakly. "I'll be dead soon."

"Why were you trying to kill us?"

"Doesn't matter."

Becca joined the SEALs huddled around the man on the deck. "His name is Trey Danner. Former FBI. Since being fired from that job, he's gone rogue and has been hiring out to the highest bidder."

"Doing what?" Jenna asked. "Killing people?"

Becca nodded. "He's a mercenary."

Danner shrugged, the movement making him wince and then cough. Blood trickled from the corner of his mouth. "It pays better than flipping burgers."

Duff stepped forward, his fists clenched. "Bastard."

Lance nodded. "He's the guy we saw in the video of

the lobby. The one who came to the concierge desk after Jenna took the case."

"I ran into him in the resort lobby," Jenna shivered. "So he was supposed to receive the case with the sniper rifle."

Danner closed his eyes. "Don't know what you're talking about." He coughed and lay still.

"Who hired you?" Duff dropped to a knee beside the injured man.

"Dead men don't tell secrets…" Danner whispered, his words barely understandable.

Duff reached for the man's shoulders and shook him. "Who the hell hired you to kill Sawyer?"

Montana laid a hand on Duff's shoulder. "Let's get him fixed up, and then we can interrogate him."

Duff released his hold and stood.

Quentin pressed two fingers to the base of Danner's throat. "I don't think there will be any fixin'. This guy's dead."

Lance hurried up the steps into the helm. Before long he had turned the vessel toward Cancún, radioing ahead for an ambulance to meet them at the dock.

While Carly kept pressure on the belly wound around the knife, Jenna held Sawyer's hand in hers, praying he'd stay alive long enough to get to medical help.

Sawyer looked up at her, his eyes glazed, his face pale. "I swear I'll be okay." His voice faded and his eyelids drooped closed.

Jenna glanced up to see Natalie, Montana, Duff and Quentin surrounding Becca.

Duff tilted his head toward Natalie, his eyes narrow. "You'd better question her. I'm not in the mood to be nice."

Natalie's lips curved briefly as she faced Becca. Her expression sobered and she stared at the woman, all trace of humor gone. "Why are you here and why did you know so much about Danner?"

Becca straightened, throwing back her shoulders. "I've been following Danner."

"Why?" Quentin shot at her.

"He killed someone I cared about," Becca said, her voice strong, her chin tilting.

"Who?"

She took a deep breath, her eyes glazing. "My father."

"And what makes you qualified to chase mercenaries?" Natalie asked.

Becca's lips quirked. "Same thing that makes you qualified to go after him."

Lance called down from above. "Natalie, Royce said not to shoot Becca. She's one of us."

Becca smiled. "You've been away for two years." She stuck out her hand to Natalie. "Welcome back to SOS."

Natalie took the hand, her brows furrowed. "You must have come on board after I left."

"That's right," Becca said. "I've heard a lot about you."

Sawyer's eyes blinked open, and he stared up at Jenna. "Did I hear that right? She's an agent?"

Jenna touched his face. "You heard right. Apparently she works with the same agency as Lance and Natalie."

Becca's smile faded. "The difference is, I have a stake in the outcome of this case."

"Revenge?" Duff slipped an arm around Natalie's waist.

"No." Becca crossed her arms. "Justice. I refuse to let the man who killed my father get away with murder."

"Well, you got what you came for," Quentin said.

Becca shook her head. "Almost. But not quite. You heard Danner. Someone hired him to kill Sawyer and Devita. I'll bet whoever hired him to kill those two was also responsible for killing my father."

"The question is, what is the connection between your father, Devita and Sawyer?" Duff asked.

Jenna gripped Sawyer's hand. "The note said to bring Sawyer Houston to a certain location, dead or alive."

"Which leads me to think they were going to use him to lure his father to Cancún."

"And since they didn't care if he was dead or alive, they probably weren't after Sawyer for a ransom."

"I'm still here," Sawyer said. "Not dead."

Jenna chuckled. "Stay with us. We'll figure this out."

Sawyer squeezed Jenna's hand and turned his head toward Natalie, Becca and the others. "My father's on his way to Cancún, despite my request that he not come."

Becca drew in a deep breath and let it out. "Whoever hired Trey could have more than one mercenary working for him. When Senator Houston arrives, he could be the next target."

Sawyer tried to sit up but fell back, wincing. "Got to get to him first."

Jenna laid a hand on his shoulder. "You'll be in the hospital. You're not going anywhere."

"But we can meet him," Duff said. "And equip him with some body armor before he heads to the hospital to visit his son."

Becca shook her head. "The man's a moving target. The man who killed my father and Devita is ruthless. He probably wants the senator to suffer and will kill his son first. Then he'll stop at nothing to kill the senator."

Jenna's mind raced ahead, her thoughts processing all the pieces. "Then we have to kill Sawyer and let the man who wants the senator dead have the senator killed."

Sawyer frowned up at her. "I thought you liked me."

Jenna smiled down at him. "Don't you see? Whoever

wants the senator to suffer won't kill him until he watches his son die."

"My father doesn't give a damn about whether I live or die," Sawyer said softly. "But I kind of like living, if you don't mind."

"So we fake your death, which brings your father to the hospital. When he leaves the hospital, we assassinate him."

"I can go along with a fake death—ideally it'll only be fake." Sawyer's frown deepened. "But though I don't get along with my father, I don't want him to die."

"Yeah, neither do we." Becca tapped her chin. "But until we find out who is behind all these killings, your father needs to fake his death and go into some kind of witness protection program. Otherwise, he'll continue to be a target of this madman."

"Royce can set up the witness protection program," Natalie said.

Becca nodded. "He's done it before. And it might be better if he does. I have a feeling the man behind these assassination attempts is or was someone in a government agency."

"Why?" Jenna asked.

"My father was a member of the CIA working with the DEA on a drug-trafficking case involving Devita."

"How does Sawyer's father fit into this?" Duff asked.

Becca's brows drew together. "I'm not sure, but my father mentioned having meetings with Senator Houston on several occasions."

Sawyer's fingers tightened around Jenna's. "My father was on the Subcommittee for Terrorism, Drug Trafficking and International Operations." He spoke with his eyes closed, his grip weakening. "Now, if you'll excuse me, I think I'll sleep."

His hand went limp in Jenna's. She leaned forward,

touched her fingers to the base of his neck and held her breath. The weak but steady thump of his pulse gave her only a brief feeling of relief. If they didn't get him to a hospital soon, he'd bleed out.

The lights of Puerto Cancún made the sky glow as the yacht turned into the port's channel.

"We need to prepare for boarding." Natalie nodded to the men. "Gather anything and everything to do with weapons and ammunition and stash it in the safe room below."

Montana, Duff and Quentin sprang into action. Carly, Natalie and Becca followed. Before they pulled into the slip at the marina, every weapon and all the ammo and casings had been policed and stored in the hidden room on the lower level. The men had scrubbed their faces clean of the camouflage paint and brought a damp cloth for Jenna to clean the paint off Sawyer's face.

Strobe lights on emergency vehicles blinked on the road beside the marina.

As the yacht pulled in, Mexican police swarmed the decks, followed by emergency medical technicians carrying a stretcher.

Careful not to jostle the knife in Sawyer's belly, they loaded him onto the stretcher, started an IV and affixed an oxygen mask to his face.

"I'm going with him," Jenna insisted.

"Are you a relative?" one of the technicians asked in heavily accented English.

"I'm his fiancée," she lied. She didn't want to let Sawyer out of her sight. There might be other hired mercenaries wandering around Cancún. She refused to let them have a clear shot at Sawyer.

"We'll be right behind you," Duff reassured her. "We won't let anything happen to him."

Before Jenna could climb into the back of the ambulance with Sawyer, Natalie touched her arm. "We'll get my boss to contact Sawyer's father before he lands in Cancún and set the plan in motion."

Jenna nodded. "Thank you. Let me know if I can help in any way. Otherwise I'll be at Sawyer's bedside."

Natalie stared at her for a long moment. "You already know what has to happen."

"I do," Jenna said.

Natalie, Becca, Carly and Lance would stay behind and answer questions about Trey's death, claiming he was the victim of a terrible boat wreck, which was the truth.

"I'll be outside the room to provide protection," Duff said. "Sawyer's like a brother to me."

"And me," Montana added.

"And me," Quentin agreed.

Jenna climbed into the back of the ambulance and smiled at the SEALs. "He's lucky to have you."

"Damn right he is." Duff winked and jogged to the battered Jeep in the parking lot. Quentin and Montana hurried after him.

Jenna hoped they remembered to fill the radiator with water before they started the engine on the bullet-riddled rental car.

She sat as far forward and out of the way as possible so that the medical technician had access to work on Sawyer, if needed. She was comforted whenever she caught glimpses of the Jeep following them to the hospital.

Sawyer didn't awaken.

When they reached the hospital, he was taken directly into surgery.

Duff, Montana and Quentin joined Jenna in the waiting room.

The scent of disinfectant brought back memories of

being in the hospital with her mother as she lay dying of cancer. The last time she had held her mother's hand, Jenna had been twelve.

Her throat constricted and her fists clenched. Sawyer would not die. He couldn't. Though they'd only just met and spent two nights making love, their chemistry was off the charts. Jenna knew Sawyer was special, compassionate and the kind of guy who would never leave a woman standing alone at the altar. He was a man of his word, a man of integrity and grit.

Her father would approve of Sawyer and welcome him into the family, if anything came of their relationship.

She brushed a tear from her eye, shaking her head at how far ahead of herself she was getting. Sawyer had to make it through the operation first. Then, if he was interested, she hoped they could go on a real date. Maybe relax on the beautiful beaches of Cancún without being shot at or stabbed.

If he didn't want to continue seeing her, she'd understand. But damn. She hoped he would consider it.

"Are you all right?" Duff asked.

Jenna stared up at the big SEAL. His jaw was tight. "I'm okay. Just worried about Sawyer."

Duff nodded. "He's been through worse and come out all right."

She smiled. "I believe it."

"Natalie just texted. Her boss was able to get through to Senator Houston. He landed fifteen minutes ago. Natalie is going to meet him at the airport and prepare him."

Jenna drew in a deep breath and let it out slowly. "And so it begins."

Neither Sawyer nor his father was out of the woods yet. Though mercenary Trey Danner was dead, they couldn't be certain others wouldn't come along and try to kill the Houstons.

Finally a man in scrubs entered the waiting room, pulling a surgical mask from his face. "Senor Houston is fine. The shoulder wound will heal nicely, no serious damage to his muscles or bones. The knife missed all major organs. However, he lost a considerable amount of blood. We wish to monitor him overnight."

A nurse led them to a private hospital room, where Sawyer lay against the crisp white sheets, an IV attached to his arm, monitors checking his pulse and heartbeat. Though his face was pale, he appeared to be resting easy.

"He should come out of the anesthesia soon," the nurse said.

After Sawyer's teammates had a chance to see their buddy, they left Jenna alone with him. She sat in the chair beside his bed, holding his hand. The sun had come up two hours ago, but the activities that had occurred over the past couple of days weighed heavily on Jenna's eyelids. Eventually she leaned her head against the mattress and slipped into a deep sleep.

LIGHT EDGED BETWEEN Sawyer's eyelids, forcing him awake. Though he tried to open his eyes, he struggled to perform the simple action. His limbs felt heavy and his belly hurt, as if someone had stabbed a knife in his gut.

Knife. Attack.

Sawyer jerked awake, his eyes flew open and he tried to sit up. Pain forced him to reconsider, and he lay back against the sheet.

Something soft and silky brushed against his arm. When he glanced down, his heart swelled.

Jenna, the woman who'd risked her life to save him by jumping onto the back of a WaveRunner, was asleep with her head lying on the mattress of the hospital bed, her hand next to his.

This woman had done more for him than any stranger ever would. Boring she was not. *Caring, passionate, brave* and *beautiful* described her. Sawyer believed he knew her better in the short time he'd known her than her ex-fiancé had. Hell, the man probably never tried to get to know her properly. When he got out of the hospital and no one was gunning for him, he'd take Jenna on a real date, treating her to dinner, dancing and the romance she deserved.

He smoothed a hand over her auburn hair, wishing she would wake and let him see her bright green eyes. But she was so peaceful and getting some much-needed sleep after the events of the night before.

Jenna stirred and lifted her head, those green eyes shining up at him sleepily. "You're awake."

He chuckled and winced. "I am. How long have I been out?"

She glanced around the room, shaking her head. "I have no idea."

"Before everything starts getting crazy, I wanted to say thank-you."

Her brows crinkled and her lips twisted. "For what?"

"For being the brave, beautiful and exciting woman you are." He brushed a strand of silken hair back behind her ear. "And for saving my life."

She shook her head. "You almost died last night."

"But I didn't. And you saved my life in more ways one."

"What do you mean?" she asked, smoothing her hand over the sheet, her lashes dropped to mask her expression.

Sawyer lifted her chin with one finger, forcing her to look at him. "You reminded me there is more to life than work and I don't have to be a cold bastard like my father."

"Never cold," she said, her fingers linking with his.

"You have a big heart, Sawyer. Your teammates would vouch for that."

"And you?"

She tilted her head. "My instincts say you have a big squishy heart, but I have a problem trusting my instincts. I'd really like to get to know you better. Spend some time with you. But that's completely up to you. You might not even like me."

He snorted. "Not a chance. I think I could really come to love you."

Jenna's eyes widened.

The *L* word coming out of Sawyer's mouth was almost as shocking to him as it was to Jenna, based on her expression. "Wow, did I really say that?"

She nodded. "You did. And you can't take something like that back."

He cupped her cheek. "I don't want to. As I see it, I have almost a week left of vacation and you just got here. I don't suppose you'd want to go out with a man who has stitches in his belly and probably can't dance for a few weeks?"

She smiled. "I'd love to go sit by the swimming pool and soak up some sun with you. Maybe even read a book."

"You've got a date, darlin'." He tried to sit up again, the pain stabbing him in the belly forcing him to lie back. "I'd kiss you, but it seems sitting up isn't in the cards for me yet."

"Allow me." Jenna stood and leaned over the bed, brushing her lips across his.

"Mmm. That's good. But this is better." Sawyer cupped the back of her head and brought her down for a deep, soul-defining kiss that shook him to the core. When he loosened his hold on her, she swayed, her eyes glazed and her lips swollen.

"That was good," she whispered. "I hope they let you out of the hospital soon."

"Me, too." He tugged on her hand. "In the meantime, I bet there's room for both of us on this bed."

A knock on the door kept him from scooting over.

Duff leaned in. "It's time for Operation Phoenix." He stepped through the door and let it close behind him.

Sawyer frowned.

Duff glanced from Sawyer to Jenna. "Jenna didn't tell you?"

Sawyer stared at her. "Tell me what?"

"Your father landed in Cancún a little while ago. He's on his way to the hospital to see you."

Sawyer pushed himself up in the bed, grimacing to fight the pain of pulled stitches. "Damn, that hurts." Once upright, he tried to swing his legs over the side. "You have to stop him. There could be a killer out there waiting to take him out."

Duff nodded. "Yeah. We're banking on it."

"What?" Sawyer stared at his friend. Had Duff lost his mind?

"You don't remember the conversation?" Jenna's mouth twisted into a wry grin. "You were pretty much out of it. Your father needs to die long enough to let Natalie's team of special agents figure out who is behind the death of Becca's father, Devita and all of the attempts on your life, including the cut cable on the zip-line adventure."

Duff nodded. "They're going to get him to go into something like witness protection until they can nail the bastard."

"Sawyer, you really should lie down," Jenna said.

Now that he was up, the thought of lying back in the bed sounded equally as painful as sitting up. "I'm okay."

"You're bleeding through your bandages." Jenna glanced at Duff. "Help me get him to lie down."

Duff hurried to the other side of the bed. "Let us do the work for you. Jenna's right. You have to let the wounds heal." Between Jenna and Duff, they lowered him to the mattress.

Sawyer groaned. "I hate being so damn helpless."

Jenna stared down at the red stain on his belly and bit her lip. "I should call the nurse back in to have her check the damage you've done."

"I'm fine," Sawyer said. "I want to hear how you plan to get my father killed without actually hurting him."

"If the assassin doesn't try to take him out on his way in, *you* have to pretend to die while he's here so the assassin will attempt a hit on his life on the way out." Duff raised his hands. "What? You don't like the plan?"

"What if the killer succeeds?"

"Your father will be outfitted with armor plates."

"What about his head?" Sawyer asked. "If the assassin is worth anything, he could aim for the head. Did you give my father a helmet?"

Duff grinned. "No, but we gave him a Kevlar fedora."

Sawyer shook his head. "A what?"

Duff's grin widened. "Natalie's boss has some amazing connections."

"I still don't like the idea of my father coming here. I don't know why he's here. He never came to anything when I was growing up. Hell, he didn't come to my graduation from BUD/S training."

"Maybe he's finally coming around," Duff said.

Jenna tightened her hold on his hand. "I'm going to run to the restroom and grab a cup of coffee, if I can find a cafeteria."

"I'll stay with him until you get back."

"I don't need a damn babysitter," Sawyer groused.

"No, but you're in no condition to fight off an attack."

"Danner's dead."

"You want to bank your life that there's not another man waiting to do the job Danner couldn't?" Duff asked.

Jenna headed for the door. "I'll let you two duke this one out. I'll be back as soon as possible."

The door closed behind her, leaving Duff and Sawyer alone.

"She's feisty," Duff said.

Sawyer's gaze remained on the door Jenna had disappeared through. "Yes. She is." His lips curled upward. "I like that about her."

Duff stared at Sawyer. "Look at the two of us."

"What?" Sawyer frowned up at his friend.

"You and me. Confirmed bachelors, determined to stay that way. 'A SEAL has no right to drag a female into his life.'" Duff chuckled. "Remember saying that?"

Sawyer thought about it. "Yeah. I do remember saying that. And it's still true."

"What if the woman is fully aware of your profession? Haven't you ever thought it might be up to the woman to make that decision?"

Sawyer chewed on Duff's words. "I guess."

Duff raised his hands, palms up. "We should let them make that choice rather than making it for them."

"Seems kind of selfish to want someone and not be there for them." He tapped the mattress with his fingers. "Like how my father made the choice to marry and have children, then more or less abandoned us to his career."

"How many times do I have to tell you that you're not your father?" Duff paced toward the window, performed an about-face and paced back. "You deserve to be happy. And if the female you care about loves you enough to take you, career and all, she deserves the chance to make that decision for herself."

Sawyer stared at his friend, his eyes narrowing. "Are you trying to convince me or yourself?"

"You, brother." Duff walked to the window again and shot a glance over his shoulder. "I'm already convinced."

"You found the perfect woman for you."

"And you haven't?"

Sawyer's gaze remained on the closed door. "Maybe."

"Then give her and yourself a chance. You said it yourself. She's feisty." Duff turned to stare out the window. "She'll need to be to put up with you."

"Jerk."

Duff didn't respond. His body tensed and he leaned toward the glass. "If I'm not mistaken, your father is in the parking lot and headed for the front entrance."

Sawyer tried to sit up again, but the pain in his abdomen was too much. "What's happening?"

"Well, he's wearing the fedora, and judging from the bulky way he looks in his suit, he's decked out in the armor plating."

"What's going on?" Sawyer demanded.

"Nothing so far."

Sawyer didn't like this. "Get me up. I want to see what's going on."

"No way. You're bleeding— Holy hell!" Duff said. "He's down!"

Again, Sawyer forced himself to a sitting position, the stitches ripping his skin. Warm blood trickled, filled the white bandages and dripped down his belly. When he slipped out of the bed and tried to stand, he almost passed out.

"What the hell are you doing?" Duff was at his side in

an instant, lifting him up and settling him in the bed. "I'm going to get a nurse in here."

"Don't. I'd rather you went to my father and helped him. Armored plates don't cover the entire body."

Duff shot a glance toward the window. "You gotta promise me you won't do something stupid while I'm gone, like trying to join me."

"I'll stay here. But I need to know you're looking out for my father."

"On it." Duff ran for the door and turned at the last second. "SEAL's honor."

Sawyer held up a hand. "SEAL's honor."

Duff left, and the door swung closed behind him.

Unable to sit still while his father could be in trouble, Sawyer swung his legs out of the bed. This time he held on when he got out and waited for his head to clear. He must have lost a lot of blood. He felt as weak as a newborn. But somehow he made it to the window and stared down at the gathering crowd around his father. He could make out Montana, Quentin, Natalie, Lance and Becca. Even Carly was down there, helping make sure the killer believed Senator Houston was dead.

Duff joined them and helped the hospital staff lift Sawyer's father onto a gurney and wheel him into the hospital.

So intent on the drama unfolding on the ground below his window, Sawyer didn't hear the door open. He didn't hear the footsteps crossing the floor until too late.

Something grabbed his head and slammed it into the window with such force, pain shot through his skull and he dropped to the ground, the fog of unconsciousness completely enveloping him.

Chapter Sixteen

Jenna had made use of the facilities, found a café and ordered two cups of coffee. She was backing into the swinging door of Sawyer's room when she heard a loud bang on the other side.

Thinking Sawyer might have fallen out of the bed, she shoved through quickly, her gaze going to the empty bed. Then she saw the man dressed in scrubs crouched by the window with a pillow in his hand, pressing it hard over Sawyer's face.

Jenna flung the cups of hot coffee at the man and charged at him, hitting him like a linebacker tackling a quarterback. Her impact was enough force to knock him into the window glass.

He staggered, righted himself and spun to face her.

Jenna backed away and did the only other thing she could think of—she screamed bloody murder and dived across the bed, landing on the other side.

The man rounded the bed and came at her, his hands reaching for her neck.

Jenna grabbed the lamp off the nightstand and swung it hard.

The attacker knocked the lamp from her hands and it crashed into the wall.

The attacker's hands wrapped around her throat and squeezed.

Kicking and flailing with all her strength, Jenna couldn't get the man to let go. Her throat ached, she couldn't breathe and darkness crept in around the edges of her vision. All she could think of was that she couldn't let this guy kill her. If he did, there'd be no one stop him from killing Sawyer, if he hadn't already.

With renewed resolve, she jerked her knee up, connecting with the man's groin. He loosened his hold. Jenna knocked his arms away. She dropped to the ground, rolled out of reach and stood on the other side of the bed. With the little bit of strength she had left, she shoved the bed with all her might, slamming it against the man and pinning him against the wall.

Then Sawyer was standing beside her, leaning his weight into the bed with her, his face pale but his jaw set.

Trapped at the waist, the man couldn't free his legs. He reached into the waistband of his scrubs and pulled out a handgun.

A large, shiny bedpan sailed across the room and caught the gun as the man pulled the trigger. His arm jerked back.

Jenna's heart stopped. Nothing had hit her, which led her to believe Sawyer had been hit. When she looked over at him, her heart started beating again. He was still upright. The only blood visible soaked his bandages where he'd ripped his stitches loose.

Duff charged into the room and yanked the man out from between the wall and the bed, jerked his arm up behind his back and slammed his face into the wall.

Montana arrived and offered a zip tie to secure the man's wrists behind his back. "Nice to see you have things under control. While you take care of our assassin, I'll check on things downstairs."

Jenna slipped an arm around Sawyer's waist and let him lean on her.

"My father?" Sawyer asked.

Natalie entered the room as Duff left, and went to Sawyer, wrapping her arms around his neck. "Sawyer, I'm so very sorry."

"What?" Sawyer gripped her arms. "What happened?"

Jenna's heart pinched in her chest. Though she knew this was all a sham, she was amazed at how real Natalie and Sawyer made it feel.

"Your father—" Natalie paused, swallowed hard and continued "—was shot dead at the front entrance of the hospital." Then she hugged him again and whispered something into his ear. She stepped back. "They've taken him to the morgue in the basement. His body will be prepared for shipment back to the States."

Sawyer stared at her for a long time before saying, "I want to see him."

"You shouldn't be up and about," Jenna said. "You're bleeding."

"I'll let the doc sew me up again, but I want to see my father one last time."

A nurse entered with two Mexican policemen.

The policemen took the attacker out of the room.

Duff left and returned with a wheelchair. He and Jenna eased Sawyer into it. Then Duff rolled him out of the room and down the hallway to the elevator. Jenna walked beside the chair and held Sawyer's hand. She had to let go as they entered the elevator car.

The trip to the basement didn't take long. When they arrived, an orderly led them into an embalming room, where a body lay on a gurney, covered in a sheet and surrounded by Lance, Quentin, Montana, Carly and Becca.

Natalie spoke to the orderly in halting Spanish, and he left.

As soon as the door closed behind the orderly, Senator Houston flung back the sheet and sat up on the gurney. "I thought you'd never get rid of that orderly." He rubbed his chest. "I have to admit, I didn't expect it to hurt that much. But I'm damn glad I had the armor plating." He directed his attention to Sawyer, his brow furrowing into deep lines. "Son, are you okay?"

Sawyer frowned. "Why did you come?"

The frown eased from the senator's brow. "I got a message that you would be killed if I didn't come to Cancún immediately." He stared at Sawyer. "I came."

Sawyer's jaw tightened.

Jenna could feel the tension between the two men. She laid a hand on Sawyer's shoulder, wanting to take away the physical as well as the emotional pain. But she remained silent.

Sawyer reached up and covered her hand with his as he spoke to his father. "You realize now that you're dead, you have to stay dead until we figure out who is trying to kill you."

His father nodded. "I spoke with Royce Fontaine, head of Stealth Operations Specialists. I understand what has to happen."

"And you're going to walk away from your office for however long it takes?"

"For good, if I have to." Rand Houston shoved a hand through his hair. "On the flight down from DC, I had time to reflect on my life, yours and what's important. It took me thirty years to come to the conclusion that your life is more important to me than my work in the senate."

Sawyer snorted. "A little late, don't you think?"

His father nodded. "Yeah. But not too late for you. Now

that I'm playing dead, whoever wanted to hurt me by hurting you ideally will stop trying. That's what counts. Look, son, I don't expect you to forgive me for being a lousy father. I just want you to live a full life and be happy. If being a SEAL makes you happy, I think that's great. I might not have told you this, but the proudest day of my life was the day you graduated BUD/S training. I couldn't be there because we had a hostage crisis in Libya going on at the time." The senator shook his head. "I know. It was always something. I'm glad you're going to be okay, and I hope when this is all over, we can meet for coffee and start over." He held out his hand to his son.

For a long moment, Sawyer stared at it. Finally he took the hand and shook it. "I'll take you up on that cup of coffee as long as I get to choose the place. I can't stand that fancy coffee."

Senator Houston grinned. "You're on."

Natalie's cell phone buzzed. She listened and then lifted her head. "Senator Houston, your ambulance has arrived to take you to the plane."

He nodded and looked around the room as if for the first time. "I guess I'm off to a new life and a new identity. Who knows? Maybe I'll like it enough that I won't want to go back to the Capitol." He lay back on the gurney. Natalie covered him with the sheet, and they rolled him out of the morgue, into the waiting ambulance.

Quentin and Montana rode in the back of the ambulance with the senator. Carly opted to go with Quentin.

Once his father was on his way to the airport, Sawyer let Duff push his wheelchair back to the elevator and help him to his room and the bed.

"If you're all right, I think I'll head to the hotel with Natalie and Becca. I'd like to get a shower and shave. I'll be back later."

Sawyer waved at his friend. "Go. I seriously doubt I'll be attacked again. If I am, I have my bodyguard to keep me safe." He smiled at Jenna.

A warm feeling spread through her, but it was immediately cooled when the nurse and doctor entered the room.

They spent the next ten minutes suturing the torn stitches. They gave him a bag of ice for the knot on his head from being slammed into the window and apologized for the lapse in hospital security that allowed a madman to attack him.

All the while the nurse and doctor worked with Sawyer, Jenna hung back. Now that Sawyer was on the mend and out of danger of being shot or stabbed, he no longer needed her.

Jenna wondered if she should go back to her room and get on with her vacation.

The door closed behind the doctor and nurse, leaving her alone with Sawyer.

"Hey," Sawyer said. "Why are you way over there, when I'm way over here?"

Jenna shrugged. "I was thinking I should go, now that you don't need me anymore."

"What are you talking about?" He lay back against the pillows. "You're my bodyguard. All you need is a couple of cups of coffee and a hospital bed to neutralize any threat."

Jenna crossed to him and let him take her hand. She liked the way it looked so small in his bigger hand. "I figured you might not want a boring accountant holding you back."

He caught her chin in his palm and forced her to look at him. "You are not boring. Hell, you're the most exciting woman I've ever had the honor to be saved by." He laced his fingers with hers and brought them to his lips. "A wise old SEAL told me I should give myself and my girl a chance to find happiness. Now, since I don't have a girl, or at least don't have one yet, I was hoping, if you can stand to be around a guy who is all cut up and might bleed on you while making love, you might consider going on a date with me?"

Her heart swelled and threatened to burst from her chest. "I'd love to."

"Good. As soon as I'm out of this hospital, you're on. But while I'm stuck here, I swear this bed will fit two." He patted the mattress beside him. "I won't ask for anything but your warm body next to mine, and I'll even let you sleep, because—" he yawned "—I think they gave me a really good painkiller."

Jenna crawled up beside him, careful not to jolt him. Then she lay in the curve of his arm, snuggling beside a pretty amazing SEAL.

"Mmm. Now, that's more like it," Sawyer murmured. "I could fall in love with a woman like you. Feisty and never boring."

* * * * *

Read on for an excerpt from
HARD RAIN,
the next installment in
New York Times *bestselling author*
B.J. Daniels's series
THE MONTANA HAMILTONS.

When Brody McTavish sees Harper Hamilton's runaway
horse galloping across the pastures, he does what any
good cowboy would do—gives chase and rescues her. But
they soon have bigger problems when they make a grue-
some discovery—human remains that will dredge up old
Hamilton family mysteries...and bring about a scandal
that could threaten all Harper's loved ones.

CHAPTER ONE

*Thunder cracked overhead in a piercing boom that rat-
tled the windows. As she huddled in the darkness, rain
pelted down in angry drenching waves. Lightning again
lit the sky in a blinding flash that burned in her mind the
image before her.*

*In that instant, she saw him crossing the field carry-
ing the shovel, his head down, rain pouring off his black
Stetson. It was done.*

*Dark clouds blanketed the hillside. Through the driving
rain, she watched him come toward her, telling herself she
could live with what she'd done. But she feared he could
not. And that could be a problem.*

BRODY MCTAVISH HEARD the screams only seconds before
he heard the roar of hooves headed in his direction. Shoving back his cowboy hat, he looked up from the fence he'd
been mending to see a woman on a horse riding at breakneck speed toward him.

Harper Hamilton. He'd heard that she'd recently returned after being away at college. Which meant it could
have been years since she'd been on a horse. He was already grabbing for his horse's reins and swinging up in
the saddle.

Runaway horse.

He'd been on a runaway horse when he was a kid. He
remembered how terrifying it had been. With that many

pounds of horseflesh running at such a deadly speed, he prayed hard she could hang on.

He had to hand it to Harper. She hadn't been unseated. At least not yet.

Harper, yards away on a large bay, screamed. He spurred his horse to catch her and as he raced up beside her, her blue eyes were wide with alarm.

Acting quickly, he looped an arm around her, dragged her off the horse and reined in. His horse came to a stop in a cloud of dust. Her horse kept going, disappearing into the foothill pines ahead.

Brody let Harper slip to the ground next to his horse. The minute her feet touched earth, she started screaming again as if all the wind had been knocked out of her when he'd grabbed her but was back now.

"You're all right," he said, swinging out of the saddle and stepping to her to try to calm her.

She spun on him, leading with her fist, and caught him in the jaw. He staggered back more from surprise than the actual blow, but the woman had a pretty darned good right hook.

He stared at her in confusion. "What the devil was that about?"

Picking up a baseball-sized rock, she brandished it as she took a few steps back from him, all the time glancing around, seeming either to expect more men to come out of the foothills, or looking for a larger weapon.

Had the woman hit her head? He spoke as calmly as he would to a skittish horse—or a crazy woman. "Calm down. I know you're scared. But you're all right now." It had only been a few months since the two of them were attendants at her sister Bo's wedding, not that they hadn't known each other for years.

She peered under the brim of his hat as if only then taking a good look at him. "Brody McTavish?" She stared at him as if in shock. "Have you lost your mind?"

Brody frowned, since this hadn't been the reaction he'd expected. "Ah, correct me if I'm wrong," he said, rubbing his jaw. "But I don't think this is the way most women would react after a man saves her life."

"You think you just saved my life?" Her voice rose in amazement.

"You were *screaming* like either a woman in trouble or one who has lost her senses. I assumed, as any sane person would, that your horse had run away with you. No need to thank me," he said sarcastically.

"Thank you? For scaring me half to death?" She dropped the rock and dusted the dirt off her hand onto her jeans. "And for the record, I wasn't *screaming.* I was…expressing myself."

"Expressing yourself at the top of your lungs?"

Harper jammed her hands on her hips and thrust out her adorable chin. He recalled her sister's wedding back at Christmastime. While both attendants, they hadn't shared more than a few words. Nor had he gotten a chance to dance with her. His own fault. He hadn't wanted to get in line with all her young suitors.

"It was a beautiful morning," she said haughtily. "I hadn't been on a horse in a long time and it felt so good that I couldn't resist expressing it." She looked embarrassed but clearly wasn't about to admit it. "Do you have a problem with that?"

"Nope. But when I see a woman riding like a wild person, screaming her head off, I'm going to assume she's in trouble and needs some help. My mistake." Didn't she know how dangerous it was riding like that out here? If her horse had stepped into a gopher hole… A lecture came to his lips, but he clamped his mouth shut. "You have a nice day, Miss Hamilton." He tipped his hat, grabbed up his reins and started to walk back toward his property.

"You're just going to walk away?" she demanded to his back.

"Since you aren't in need of *my* help…" he said over his shoulder.

"I thought you would at least help me retrieve my horse."

He stopped and mumbled under this breath, "If your horse has any sense he'll keep going."

"I beg your pardon?"

Brody took a breath and turned to face her again.

Her blond hair shone in the morning sunlight, her blue eyes wide and filled with devilment. He recalled the girl she'd been. Feisty was an understatement. While nothing had changed as far as that went, she was definitely no longer a girl. He would have had to be blind not to notice the way she filled out her jeans and Western shirt.

She shifted her boots in the dust. "I'd appreciate it if you would help me find my horse."

"By all means let me help you find your horse then. As you said, it's the least I can do. Would you care to ride… *Miss Hamilton*?" He motioned to his horse, glad he hadn't called her *Princess*, even though it had been on the tip of his tongue.

Looking chastised, she shook her head. "And, please, my name is—"

"Harper. I know."

"Glad you didn't mistake me for my twin." She sounded more than a little surprised. "Not even my own father can tell us apart at times."

He could feel her looking at him, studying him like a bug under a microscope. He wondered what she'd majored in at college. Nothing useful, he would bet.

"Thank you for helping me find my horse," she said into the silence that fell between them. "I really don't want to be left out here on foot if my horse has returned to the barn."

He thought the walk might do her some good but was smart enough not to voice it. "The last I saw of your mare she was headed up into the foothills. I would imagine that's where we'll find her, next to the creek."

She glanced up at him. "I apologize for hitting you." When he said nothing, she continued. "With everything that's been going on in my family, I thought you were... Anyway, I'm sorry that I hit you and that I misunderstood your concern." He could hear in her voice how hard that apology was for her.

And, he had to admit, her family had recently definitely been through a lot. The family had seemed to be under attack since her father, Senator Buckmaster Hamilton, had announced he would be running for president. Three of her sisters had been threatened. Not to mention the mother she'd believed dead had returned out of the blue after twenty-two years—and her stepmother had been killed in a car accident. It was as if tragedy was tracking that family.

"Apology accepted," he said as he picked up her cowboy hat from the dust and handed it to her.

As they walked toward sun-bleached cliffs and shimmering green pines, he mentally kicked himself. He'd had a crush on Harper—from a distance, of course—for years, waiting for her to grow up, and now that she finally had and he'd managed to get her attention, he couldn't imagine a worse encounter.

Not that he wasn't knocked to his knees by her crooked smile or the way she had of cocking her head when she was considering something. Not to mention the endless blue of her wide-eyed innocence—all things he'd noticed from the first time he'd laid eyes on her. He smiled to himself, remembering the first time he'd seen her. She'd just been a freckle-faced kid.

Somehow, he'd thought… She'd be grown-up and one day… He told himself someday he and Harper would have a good laugh over this, before he mentally kicked himself.

And to think he thought he'd rescued the woman of his dreams—until she'd hit him.

BRODY MCTAVISH. HARPER grimaced in embarrassment. She'd been half in love with him as far back as she could remember. Not that he had looked twice at her. He'd been the handsome rowdy teen she used to spy on from a distance. She'd been just a girl, much too young for him. But Brody had come to parties her older sisters had put on at the ranch. She and Cassidy were too young to attend and were always sent up to bed, but Harper often sneaked down when everyone else, including her twin, thought she was asleep.

Several times Brody had caught her watching, and she'd thought for sure he would snitch on her, but he hadn't. Instead, he'd given her a grin and covered for her. Her nine-year-old heart had beat like a jackhammer in her chest at just the thought of that grin.

She'd seen Brody a few times after that, but only in passing. He'd graduated from high school and gone off to college before coming back to the ranch. She'd been busy herself, getting an education, traveling, experiencing life away from Montana. When she'd heard that her sister Bo was dating Jace Calder, she'd wondered if he and Brody were still best friends.

It wasn't until the wedding that she got to see him again. She hadn't been surprised to find that he was still handsome, still had that same self-deprecating grin, still made her now grown-up heart beat a little faster. She'd waited at the wedding reception for him to ask her to dance since they were both attendants, but he hadn't. She'd told herself that he probably still saw her as a child, given the difference in their ages.

Glancing over at him now, she didn't even want to consider what he must think of her after this. Not that she cared, she told herself, lifting her head and pretending it didn't matter. He probably didn't even remember the secret they had shared when she was a girl.

As they walked, though, she couldn't help studying him out of the corner of her eye. Earlier, she hadn't appreciated how strong he was. Now that she knew he wasn't some predator who had been trying to abduct her—something she'd been warned about since she was the daughter of a wealthy rancher and US senator—she took in his muscled body along with the chiseled features of his handsome face in the shade of his straw cowboy hat.

No matter what he said, he hadn't accepted her apology. He was still angry with her. She'd given him her best smile when he'd returned her hat from the ground and all she'd gotten was a grunt. Her smile was all it usually took with most men. But Brody wasn't most men. Wasn't that why she'd never been able to forget him?

"I feel as if we have gotten off on the wrong foot," she said, trying to make amends.

Another grunt without even looking at her.

"My fault entirely," she said, although she didn't really believe that was true and hoped he would agree.

But he said nothing, nor would he even look at her. He was starting to irritate her. She was doing her best to make up for the misunderstanding, but the stubborn man wasn't giving her an inch.

"You can't just keep ignoring me," she snapped, digging

in her boot heels as she stopped shy of the pine-covered hillside. "Have you even heard a word I've said? If you don't look at me right this minute, Brody McTavish, I'm going to—"

He swung on her. Had she not been standing flat-footed she would have stumbled back. Instead, she was rooted to the ground as suddenly he was in her face. "I've *been* listening to you and I've *been* looking at you for years," he said, his voice deep and thick with emotion. "I've *been* waiting for you to grow up." His voice faltered as he dropped his horse's reins. "Because I've been wanting to do this since you were sixteen."

Grabbing her, he pulled her against his rock-hard body. His mouth dropped to hers. Her lips parted of their own accord, just as her arms wrapped around his neck. Her heart hammered against her ribs as he deepened the kiss and she heard herself moan.

The sudden high-pitched whinny of a horse only yards away brought them both out of the kiss in one startled movement. Turning, she could see her horse in the trees. Her first thought was that the mare had gotten into a hunter's snare, because the whinny was one of pain—or alarm.

Brody grabbed her arm as she started past him to see what was wrong with her horse. "I think you should wait here," he said, letting go of her arm as he took off toward the pines.

"My horse—"

"Stay here," he said more sternly over his shoulder.

Still stunned by the kiss and anxious about her horse, she set off after him. The ground was soft under her feet. She saw where fresh soil had washed down through the pines, forming a dark, muddy gully.

Her horse was partway up the hillside near where the rain a few nights ago had loosened the soil and washed it down the hillside. As Brody approached, the mare snorted and crow-hopped away a few feet.

"She's afraid of you," she called to his retreating backside. She could hear him speaking softly to the horse as he approached. She followed, although she was no match for his long legs.

An eerie quiet fell over the hillside as she stepped into the shadowed pines. She slowed, frowning as she finally got a good look at her horse. The mare didn't seem to be hurt and yet Harper had never seen her act like this before.

"I thought I told you to stay back," Brody said as she came up behind him. "You've never been good at following orders, have you?"

So he did remember her sneaking downstairs at her sisters' parties. She felt a bump of excitement at that news, but it was quickly doused. Past him, she saw that her horse's eyes were wild. The mare snorted again, stomped the ground and shied away, to move a few yards back from them and the gully.

"What is wrong with her?" Harper demanded, afraid it was something she had done.

"She's reacting to what the hard rain dislodged and sent down the hillside in an avalanche of mud," Brody snapped. What was he talking about? As she started to step past him to get a look, he put a hand out to stop her. "Harper, you don't want to see this."

She *did* want to see whatever it was and resented him telling her she didn't. Protective was one thing, but the man was being ridiculous. She'd been raised on a ranch. She'd seen her share of dead animals, if that was what it was. She stepped around him, determined to see what the storm had exposed.

At first all she saw were old, grimy, weathered boards that looked like part of a large wooden box. Then she saw what must have been inside the container before it had washed down the slope and broken open.

Her pulse jumped at the sight, her mind telling her she wasn't seeing what her eyes told her she saw. *"What is that?"* she whispered into the already unnerving quiet as she took a step back.

"From the clothing and long hair, I'd say it was the mummified body of a woman who, until recently, had been buried up on that hillside."

Find out what happens next in
HARD RAIN by New York Times
bestselling author B.J. Daniels.
Available now wherever
HQN Books and ebooks are sold.
www.Harlequin.com

SPECIAL EXCERPT FROM

H HARLEQUIN®

INTRIGUE

Read on for a sneak peek at ALLEGIANCES,
the conclusion of **THE BATTLING McGUIRE BOYS**
by New York Times *bestselling author*
Cynthia Eden

In order to save his ex-wife, Celia, PI Sullivan McGuire
is forced to resurrect old demons. New dangers—and
dormant desires—bring Sully and Celia close...and old
enemies even closer.

"Hello, Sullivan."

At that low, husky voice—a voice Sullivan had heard far too many times in his dreams—his head whipped up. He blinked, sure that he had to be imagining the figure standing in his office doorway. He even shook his head, as if that small movement could somehow make the woman before him vanish.

Only she didn't vanish.

She laughed, and the small movement made her short red hair brush lightly against her delicate jaw. "No, sorry, you can't blink or even wish me away. I'm here." Celia James stepped inside and shut the door behind her.

He rose to his feet in a quick rush. "I wouldn't wish you away." Just the opposite. His voice had sounded too gruff, so he cleared his throat. He didn't want to scare her away, not when he had such plans for her. *And she's actually here. Close enough to touch.* "Should you... should you be here? You were hurt—"

Celia waved that injury away with a flick of her hand.

"A flesh wound. I've had worse." Sadness flickered in her eyes. "It's Elizabeth who took the direct hit. I was afraid for a while…but I heard she's better now."

He nodded and crept closer to her. Elizabeth Snow was the woman his brother Mac—MacKenzie—intended to marry as fast as humanly possible. Elizabeth was also the woman who'd been shot recently—when she faced off against a killer who'd been determined to put Elizabeth in the ground.

Only Elizabeth hadn't died, and that particular case… it had brought Celia back into Sullivan's life.

Now I can't let her leave.

He schooled his expression as he said, "She's out at the ranch. And I'm sure Mac is about to drive her crazy." He was absolutely certain of that fact. "I think his protective instincts kicked into overdrive." *So did mine. When I saw you on the ground…*

"I came to make you a deal," Celia said as she took a step toward him.

His head tilted to the side as he studied her. "A deal?" Now he was curious. Celia wasn't exactly the type to make deals. She was the type to keep secrets. The type to always get the job done, no matter what.

During Sullivan's very brief stint with the CIA, he'd met the lovely Celia.

And he'd fallen hard for her.

Until I thought she'd betrayed me.

Find out what happens in ALLEGIANCES by New York Times bestselling author Cynthia Eden.

Available May 2016 wherever Harlequin® Intrigue books and ebooks are sold.
www.Harlequin.com

HIEXP0416R

Turn your love of reading into rewards you'll love with

Harlequin My Rewards

**Join for FREE today at
www.HarlequinMyRewards.com**

Earn **FREE BOOKS** of your choice.

Experience **EXCLUSIVE OFFERS** and contests.

Enjoy **BOOK RECOMMENDATIONS**
selected just for you.

PLUS! Sign up now
and get **500** points
right away!

Earn
FREE
REWARDS
Join
Today!
HarlequinMyRewards.com

MYR16R

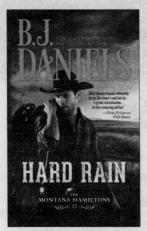

THE WORLD IS BETTER WITH

Romance

Harlequin has everything from contemporary, passionate and heartwarming to suspenseful and inspirational stories.

Whatever your mood,
we have a romance just for you!

HARLEQUIN®

A *Romance* FOR EVERY MOOD™

JUST CAN'T GET ENOUGH?

Join our social communities
and talk to us online.

You will have access to the latest
news on upcoming titles and special
promotions, but most importantly,
you can talk to other fans about your
favorite Harlequin reads.

Harlequin.com/Community

 Facebook.com/HarlequinBooks

 Twitter.com/HarlequinBooks

 Pinterest.com/HarlequinBooks